"Thomas!"

The urgency in Elizabeth's voice made his blood run cold. Had that man returned? He raced toward the back of the barn. When he cleared the open doorway, he skidded to a stop.

Elizabeth stood to his right, leaning heavily against the barn wall.

Thomas shot a hurried glance in every other direction, trying to find the danger or intruder, but saw nothing. His heart squeezed at how fragile and small and scared Elizabeth looked. Her body trembled and the piece of paper she held in her hand rattled.

"Elizabeth? What's wrong?"

The blood had drained from her face. She was almost as white as the paper. Fear widened her eyes and she didn't speak. Shakily, she held out the note.

He slid it from her fingers. Anger coursed through his body when he read the words: "I want what is mine. I will contact you again soon with a time and place to meet. Tell no one. I warn you, give it to me or die."

"I won't let anyone harm you," Thomas assured her.

Diane Burke is an award-winning author who has had seven books published with Love Inspired Suspense. She won first place in the Daphne du Maurier Award for Excellence in Mystery and Suspense and finaled in the ACFW Carol Award for book of the year. When she isn't writing, she enjoys taking walks with her dog, reading and spending time with friends and family. She loves to hear from readers and can be reached at diane@dianeburkeauthor.com. She can also be found on Twitter and Facebook.

Books by Diane Burke

Love Inspired Suspense

Midnight Caller
Double Identity
Bounty Hunter Guardian
Silent Witness
Hidden in Plain View
The Marshal's Runaway Witness
The Amish Witness

THE AMISH WITNESS

DIANE BURKE

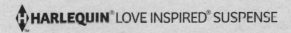

HARLEQUIN® LOVE INSPIRED® SUSPENSE

Recycling programs for this product may not exist in your area.

LOVE INSPIRED BOOKS

ISBN-13: 978-0-373-67847-1

The Amish Witness

Copyright © 2017 by Diane Burke

www.Harlequin.com

Printed in U.S.A.

We give great honor to those who endure
under suffering. For instance, you know about Job,
a man of great endurance. You can see how the Lord
was kind to him at the end, for the Lord is
full of tenderness and mercy.

–James 5:11

To my granddaughter, Emberleigh Valcich.
You are deeply loved.

ONE

Elizabeth Lapp couldn't distinguish anything out of the ordinary in the shrouded stillness of the empty Amish landscape. She lifted her kerosene lamp closer to the windowpane, pressing her face against the cool glass, and stared harder. Still nothing but dark winter shadows sheltered by even darker ones stretching across the Lancaster farm.

He was out there.

She knew it.

If not today, tomorrow or the next day, but he'd be there. Every instinct told her he would come. She'd seen him standing over Hannah's dead body—and he'd seen her.

He'd come. If only to silence her...

Dear Lord, please keep me safe. Bless me with inner peace and wisdom as I face the days ahead. And thank You, Lord, for leading me home.

The first glow of morning sun would not touch the horizon for a few more hours. Elizabeth chastised herself. There was work to do, more than enough to occupy her mind, and she needed to get to it. Chores came early on an Amish farm, even in winters in Lancaster County, when the fields lay dormant under drifts of waist-high snow.

A finger of light from the quarter moon was the only thing illuminating the distance between the house and the barn. She studied the shadows. She dared one of them to move and prayed in the same moment that none would.

Where was he? How much longer would she be tortured with the wait?

She raised her face from the glass.

Enough. You're going to make yourself sick. Where is your faith?

"What do you look for, Elizabeth?"

Elizabeth startled at the sound of her mother's voice. Her left hand flew to her chest. She swallowed a small gasp and spun around.

"You frightened me, *Mamm*. I didn't hear you coming."

"Don't be foolish. I come down these stairs the same time each morning to fix breakfast and begin the day." Mary Lapp came close, smoothed a strand of hair beneath her daughter's white prayer *kapp* and smiled. "Why do you stare out that window? Tell me, child, what do you hope to find out there in the darkness?"

It was what she *didn't* want to find that frightened her so.

She returned her mother's smile. "I'm not hoping to find anything, *Mamm*. I guess I'm having trouble adjusting to how dark it is here. There's always light in the city. No matter what time it is. The city never seems to sleep."

A shadow flitted across her mother's face. "Do you miss it already? Are you sorry you came home?"

"I'm just sorry I stayed away so long." Elizabeth had only arrived home yesterday afternoon, but she knew she had made the right decision to return. She placed her lamp on the table near the front door and a soft light enveloped the room.

Seven years had added a few strands of gray to her mother's hair. The small lines etched at the edges of her mouth had deepened, and now there were crow's feet at the edges of her eyes, but her mother would always be young and beautiful in her eyes.

"I don't miss the city, *Mamm*, and I'm glad to be home."

Her mother gave her a warm hug. "I'm glad you're home, too."

Sadness wiped the smile from Elizabeth's face. "I regret I wasn't here when *Daed* died. I never got the chance to say goodbye."

Her father had died two years ago of pneumonia. Her mother's eyes still carried her grief. Elizabeth hadn't learned he was sick until it was too late.

"I am sorry, too, little one. Your *daed* would have been pleased to have you home again. Maybe the Lord has told him you are here now. If he does know, I am certain your *daed* is thanking *Gott* every day." Mary playfully pinched her daughter's chin. "*Kumm.* Help me with breakfast."

Elizabeth followed her mother into the kitchen and lit two more lamps, as well as the gas fixture over the table. She stared at the long wooden table and smoothed her hand against the grain. Her father had made this table as a wedding gift for her mother over thirty years ago and it still looked brand-new. A pang of loss filled her heart. She wished she could have seen him one more time before he died.

"I don't remember your head always being lost in the clouds. Is that something you learned to do in that fancy city of yours?"

Elizabeth returned her mother's smile. "Sorry, *Mamm.* Just thinking about *Daed.* Wishing I had been here…"

"No good comes from looking behind you. We can't change the past." Her mother turned from the stove. "He never stopped loving you. Never." Her mother smiled. "And he knew you never stopped loving him. He understood your decision to leave even if he didn't agree with your choice."

Tears filled Elizabeth's eyes.

Silence stretched between them.

She remembered the last day she had seen her father. It had been an early winter morning like today and they'd been talking in the barn. She remembered his look of disappointment, the pain and loss already reflected in his eyes, and the warmth and love of his final embrace moments before she left.

"Elizabeth, please, get that head of yours out of the sky. We have chores to do."

Elizabeth nodded, gathered plates, silverware and mugs and set the table.

The delectable aroma of bacon and freshly brewing coffee teased her nostrils. Her stomach growled. Because her stomach had been too twisted in knots with dread and fear, she hadn't eaten much at dinner last night. But this morning she was hungry and nothing was going to snatch away her appetite.

"Could you gather some eggs from the henhouse?" her mother called over her shoulder from her spot at the propane-powered stove.

"If I can bring in a jar of your strawberry jam from the pantry to smother on your homemade bread I like so much."

Her mother smiled and waved her away. "*Ja. Ja.* Now go."

Elizabeth decided not to bother with a coat. From the house to the barn was such a short distance and she would only be exposed to the elements for a brief time. She threw a shawl over her shoulders, grabbed the hurricane lamp and hurried out the door. She'd barely cleared the third step down from the porch when a prickling sensation raced up her spine and froze her in place. She threw her gaze in one direction and then another. Looking. Anticipating.

Nothing.

Just a foolish girl's imagination running wild. That's what city life did to you. You don't trust anything or anyone anymore, do you?

She held the lamp high. The only sound was ice cracking on tree branches. Her feet wanted to scamper across the yard, but she forced herself to step off the final stair and walk slowly and purposely toward the barn.

Dear Lord, please help me stop being so afraid. If he had followed me, wouldn't he be here by now?

She took one final look around the yard.

Darkness covered the objects and bushes like shrouds.

She knew she was being foolish. No one in the city except her best friend, Hannah, had known she came from an Amish background. And Hannah had never told anyone. Had she?

Mental images of the tall man standing over Hannah's dead body flashed through her mind. Who was he? And why had he killed Hannah?

When she reached the barn door, she lifted the latch and swung it wide. The pitch-black interior gave her pause. Holding her lantern high, she stepped inside and moved deeper into the barn.

The pungent smells of livestock, hay and manure were a far cry from the exhaust fumes of the city, but they pinged nostalgia, reminding her she was home once again, and it felt good. The cows bawled as she approached, indicating their need for milking. She'd have to hurry with breakfast and get back out here to tend to them so her mother wouldn't have to.

The clucking sound of the hens in the chicken coop drew her back to the task at hand. She rubbed her hands together and blew warmth into them. Maybe she should have worn her coat. She opened her apron, holding it with her left hand, and reached inside the coop with her right. Soon she'd gathered enough eggs for both breakfast and a pudding recipe she had learned from one of her friends. Her mother would be surprised to discover that life among the *Englisch* hadn't been all bad. She'd learned to cook some wonderful recipes. She nudged the door to the coop closed.

It wasn't a sound that caught her attention. It was a feeling, an innate sense that she was no longer alone. She swallowed and tried to calm the wave of fear threatening to drown her.

It's nothing, Elizabeth. You've been on edge. Seeing bad men in shadows like children see animals in clouds.

But the internal scolding did little to calm her sense of unease.

The squawking and clucking of the hens in the coop gave her pause. The chickens knew it, too. She wasn't alone. Someone was standing close behind her...too close.

Taking another gulp, she clutched the apron filled with eggs to her chest and turned around.

A man, his face obscured in the darkness, loomed in the entrance to the barn.

Elizabeth gasped. "Who are you?" she asked. "What do you want?"

The stranger moved into the light and Elizabeth's heart stuttered.

It was him. The man she'd seen standing over Hannah's body.

"I want what your friend gave you. It belongs to me." The coldness in his tone froze her in place.

Elizabeth's eyes shot around the barn. Where could she run and hide? What could she use as a weapon if she was forced to protect herself?

"You know who I am, don't you?" he demanded.

Elizabeth took a step back. "No, sir, I don't. Please...leave. I don't know who you are. I don't have anything that belongs to you." She straightened her spine and tried to exude strength she didn't feel. "If you don't leave this property, I am going to send for the sheriff."

Then her deepest fear became a reality. He

moved toward her with such speed she barely had time to react.

Elizabeth's throat muscles froze and she couldn't scream. She backed up as fast as she could until her body slammed against a solid surface. Trapped against the chicken coop with nowhere to run, sheer panic raced through her veins.

No. No.

Elizabeth raised her hands to cover her face, dropping the edges of her apron. The eggs smashed on the ground and a few rolled across the floor.

Within seconds he was on her, his hands clasping her shoulders, his face inches from her own.

"You want me to leave? Then give me what's mine and I will." He shook her shoulders and banged her against the wooden piling behind her. "I'm not playing. Unless you want the same fate as your friend you will give it to me."

Spittle sprayed across her face as he screamed at her.

She kicked at his shins and tried to scramble from his grasp. "I don't know what you're talking about. Hannah didn't give me anything. Go away. Please. Leave me alone."

An almost evil sneer came over his face. "Hannah? So you do remember me." He dug his fingertips painfully into the soft flesh of her upper arms. "Don't make the same mistake she did. Just give me what's mine and we'll call it even. I'll go away and leave you to live your life in this forsaken place."

"Please, mister, I don't know what you want. I don't know who you are. Hannah didn't give me anything of yours."

He squeezed her arms harder and tears sprang to her eyes.

"She told me she did. She told me with her *dying* breath. I don't believe an Amish woman would pick that time to lie."

Trapped against the piling behind her, Elizabeth twisted in his grip. "Leave me alone!" She reached up and clawed at his eye.

He yelped in pain and for a split second he grabbed his face and released his grip on her arms.

It was all she needed. She threw herself sideways. The sudden shift in weight threw her off balance. She stumbled over his boot and fell hard against the wooden floor of the barn, the breath temporarily knocked out of her.

He stood over her, just like she'd seen him standing over Hannah. His hands moved to her throat. "She told me you had the information I need. Do you really think I'm going to let you ruin my life? Unless you give it to me, I'll have no choice but to make sure you suffer the same fate she did. Is that what you want?"

His hands squeezed her throat.

"Please…" she whispered. "I don't have anything. I don't know what you want."

"Hey! You! Get away." Another man, an Amish man by the sound of his dialect, entered the barn and ran out of the shadows straight toward them. "Leave her alone."

Out of the corner of her eye, Elizabeth saw the man grab a pitchfork and continue toward them.

The stranger gave one long, hard squeeze to her throat and whispered close to her face. "This isn't over. I'll be back. And if you know what's good for you, you'll keep your mouth shut or I will permanently shut it for you."

He turned and ran toward the barn's open back door. Just as quickly as he'd come he was gone.

Elizabeth rolled to her side, coughing, trying desperately to draw oxygen into her lungs.

The Amish man, whoever he was, had just saved her life.

Thomas King kneeled beside the woman who was crumpled in a heap on the dirt floor.

"Mrs. Lapp?"

What had happened? Who was that man and why had he attacked Mrs. Lapp?

Thomas offered a silent prayer of thanksgiving that he had arrived when he did. He came to the farm at the same time every morning since her husband had died. He wished he could devote more time to help out on her farm, but it was all he could spare from his own farm and family. Mrs. Lapp had always been grateful and appreciative of his help. His body shuddered at the thought of what might have happened if he had arrived a few minutes later.

"Mrs. Lapp?" His hands trembled as he reached for the woman. Placing his hand on her shoulder, he gently turned her toward him. "Are you all right?"

The lantern light dappled across her face.

This wasn't Mrs. Lapp.

He stared into the woman's face and a shaft of pain shot through his chest. He knew this face all too well. It was a face he'd thought he'd put out of his mind and his life forever, a face he'd once loved.

Elizabeth.

His eyes quickly scanned her from head to toe for any obvious injuries and found none. "Elizabeth?"

The shock registering in her pale blue eyes must have mirrored his.

"Thomas?"

"Are you hurt?"

She shook her head.

"What are you doing here? Who was that man?"

"What am *I* doing here? What are *you* doing here?" She sat up and then allowed him to help her to her feet. Her hand felt tiny in his and her fingers trembled despite the outer calmness she tried to display.

Elizabeth gently pulled her hand from his. She brushed dirt and pieces of hay from her dress and apron. "I don't know what you are doing here at this hour but I am glad you are. I hate to think what would have happened to me if you hadn't come when you did."

"Who was he?" Thomas glared at her. He knew his emotions were flashing across his features, but he was too surprised at what had happened, too shocked at whom it happened to, too upset to gain control. "What did he want? Why was he trying to hurt you? And what are you doing back at your *mamm*'s house?"

"Let's go inside." She threw a nervous glance over her shoulder. "I don't know if that man is still around." She took a step forward and stumbled.

Immediately, Thomas reached out, clasped her elbow and steadied her. "Are you hurt?" he asked again.

"No," she whispered. "Just shaken up." She placed her head against his chest for just a second while she steadied herself. He could smell the fresh scent of her hair despite her prayer *kapp* covering locks he knew were silky and blond. He remembered her scent, fresh soap and lemon, from their *rumspringa* days, when he'd lie awake at night and think of her.

Before she'd betrayed him.

Before she'd abandoned him.

Pain and anger washed over him. Where had she been all these years? And why was she back?

She felt small and fragile leaning against him.

He couldn't help himself. He wanted to hold her closer, tighter. Maybe if he did, she wouldn't run away this time.

But she was good at that, wasn't she? Running away. Leaving without a word.

"I'm sorry. I shouldn't have done that." She straightened and stepped away. "When I think of what could have happened if you hadn't come... if you hadn't helped." She stared at him, her eyes shimmering with tears. "*Denki*, Thomas."

What had happened between them seven years ago was ancient history. They both lived different lives now. He wouldn't let himself feel or remember or care. Not again.

But images of the man's hands around Elizabeth's throat filled him with rage. The possibility of what could have happened threatened to overpower him with a raw, primal fear. He had lost her once. He wouldn't be able to handle losing her again. Especially in such a heinous way.

Lord, everything happens in life according to Your plan. But this? Lord, help me understand and be strong enough to accept whatever Your plan entails.

TWO

"Elizabeth?" Mary Lapp called, presumably from the top of the porch steps. "Are you all right?" Her voice drifted into the barn. "Thomas, are you out there?"

"We're coming, *Mamm*." Elizabeth picked up the few unbroken eggs she was able to gather from the barn floor and started toward the house. Thomas silently followed.

As they drew closer, Mary called out, "When you didn't return with the eggs I became concerned. I thought I may have heard a commotion. Is everything all right?" Her eyes widened in alarm when she saw her daughter's face in the lantern light. "Elizabeth, you look scared to death! What happened?"

Elizabeth kept shooting glances over her shoulder and staring into the shadows as she hurried up the porch steps to the safety of the house. As she brushed past her mother and entered the house, Mary shot a questioning look his way.

"Thomas?"

He cupped the older woman's elbow with his hand. "Let's go inside, Mary, where it's warm. We'll talk there."

Without another word, Mary led the way. She set the lamp on the small wooden table inside the front door and followed the sounds of Elizabeth moving about the kitchen. Mary stood with Thomas in the doorway.

Elizabeth tried to appear calm and unflustered, but her hands shook as she tried to fill three coffee mugs without spilling any of the hot liquid, giving her away.

"Elizabeth? You're frightening me." Then she looked at Thomas. "What happened?"

"I'm not sure," he replied, his tone of voice grave. "There was a stranger in the barn when I arrived. I saw Elizabeth fall to the floor and the man put his hands around her throat..."

Mary gasped. Her hand flew to her chest and she rushed to her daughter's side. "What man? Did he hurt you? Are you okay?"

Thomas's eyes never left Elizabeth's face but he spoke to Mary. "I thought it was you. I knew you were expecting me so I didn't announce myself. When I saw what he was doing I panicked. I grabbed a pitchfork and raced over to help."

"Who is this man, Elizabeth?" Mary put her hands on Elizabeth's shoulders and turned her around. "Is that why you were staring out the window this morning into the darkness?"

Elizabeth nodded.

"How did this man find you? Do you know him?"

"No, I don't know him but—but I saw him. I saw him do something terrible. I am sure he followed me here. We are a small community, *Mamm.* You know it would be easy to find our farm once he came into town. He only had to mention my name and any Amish person would have been able to direct him."

Elizabeth collapsed into the nearest chair and hung her head. She couldn't seem to meet their eyes.

"I didn't know that Elizabeth had returned home," Thomas said into the uncomfortable silence.

"She only arrived yesterday afternoon," Mary replied. "There was no time to let you know."

"Did you tell her I *kumm* every morning to milk the cows and clean the stalls?"

"No. I—I couldn't seem to find the proper time to bring up the subject."

Thomas's eyes locked with hers. "You thought if she knew I worked this farm every day that she would run away again, didn't you?"

Mary looked away, but not before he saw a flash of guilt in her eyes. Her voice dropped an octave. "Of course not."

Before either of them could say anything more, Elizabeth spoke. "Please. Stop." She wrapped her hands around her mug, then squared her shoulders and looked directly at him. He saw the determination in her posture, the strength in her resolve. This was a different Elizabeth than the girl who had left years ago. This was a strong, independent woman staring back at him and Thomas found the changes intriguing.

"*Denki*, Thomas. I am grateful you were here to help me. I don't know what would have happened if you hadn't arrived when you did."

"Did he hurt you?" Mary asked. "Oh, my, look. Your throat is red. It will probably be badly bruised."

Elizabeth shook her head. "No. I'm okay. He frightened me. But I am fine now."

Mary gently touched her arm but asked no further questions, giving her daughter the time she needed to compose herself and tell the story in her own way.

"*Gut.*" Thomas remained standing in the doorway. "I am glad you were not hurt." He lifted his flat-brimmed winter hat, ran a hand through his blond hair and put the hat back in place. As much as he wanted an explanation, he knew it wasn't his place to demand one. His heart slammed against his chest. His lungs threatened to rob him of breath. He hadn't seen Elizabeth in years and here she was right in front of him. To think that just a minute or two longer and she might have died at the hands of a stranger in her very own barn was more than he could handle at the moment. He'd get the details later. For now, he needed distance so he could breathe. "I will leave the two of you to speak in private."

Before either of them could respond, he nodded at both women. "Excuse me. I have work waiting for me in the barn." He strode as fast as he could from the room.

He worked for over two hours, refusing to let his mind whisper one single thought. He milked the cows and prepared the containers for the local man to collect and take to market. He cleaned the stalls and pitched fresh hay with such speed and force a sweat broke out on his forehead despite the freezing temperatures of morning.

And although he fought hard to keep Elizabeth out of his thoughts, she crept in softly and slowly, like the sun was doing now with the dawn. He doused the lanterns and, pausing for a moment in the broad opening to the barn, stared at the white clapboard house.

Who was that man? And why had he tried to harm Elizabeth?

He knew it was not his business. He had no right to question her, to demand answers. Their time together had passed long ago. But he couldn't seem to let it go.

He went to the tack room and washed his hands

in the sink, then splashed water across his face and along the back of his neck.

Obviously, Elizabeth needed help. She must have come home looking for that help and trouble had followed her.

Thomas hung the wet towel on a rod, finger-combed his hair and put his hat back on. He sighed heavily.

She had to be terrified, even though she fought hard to make an outward show that she was in control and able to handle things on her own.

What had happened to her over the years? Where had she been?

It was none of his business.

She had made her choice years ago and it had not been a life with him. He had gone on and made a different life for himself. A happy life. One that had no room for her. He thought about his *kinner* and a smile caught the corners of his mouth. They were his joy. He couldn't help wanting to introduce them to Elizabeth. Foolish, he knew. But once she had been a friend…and so much more.

Thomas sighed again.

But if someone was terrorizing Elizabeth or trying to do worse, than he would have no choice. He wasn't the kind of man to walk away when someone needed help. And he would never walk away from Elizabeth when she needed him. He would be a friend to her. He would find a way to help.

Even when the shattered pieces of his heart silently wished he had never laid eyes on her again.

Elizabeth stood at the kitchen sink washing dishes when her mother came up behind her and placed a gentle hand on her shoulder. "I'm sorry, Elizabeth."

Elizabeth reached up and patted her hand. "For what? You did nothing wrong."

Mary turned Elizabeth to face her. "I'm sorry you had that frightening encounter with the stranger in the barn. I am also sorry I did not tell you sooner about Thomas. I am sure the shock of seeing him again was difficult for you."

"Why didn't you tell me, *Mamm*? Was Thomas right? Did you think I would run away again?" Elizabeth studied her mother's face. She'd known she would see Thomas sooner or later. She had tried to prepare herself for it before she returned to Sunny Creek. But she supposed no amount of preparation would have been good enough. The shock of seeing him again—leaning over her in the barn, standing in the kitchen doorway, his blond hair catching the glint of the lamp's glow— had made her heart seize despite all the self-talk and preparation that had gone before. There were no words good enough to dampen her feelings or assuage the guilt for betraying him.

"Never mind. It's all right, *Mamm*." She put an arm around Mary's waist. "Let's sit. We'll have a cup of coffee and talk this out."

"Go to the barn and ask Thomas to *kumm* in."

Elizabeth's eyes widened. That was the last thing she wanted or needed right now.

"Now that you have had time to compose yourself, you will sit and tell both of us the story of this man."

"I will tell you, *Mamm*, but I don't think we have to involve Thomas."

"Thomas is already involved. He deserves an explanation." Her mother smiled at her. "Besides, he is a smart man. He will be able to tell us what to do."

Elizabeth bristled. She'd lived independently and successfully for years. She didn't need a man, especially not Thomas, to tell her what to do.

But she was back in Amish territory and things were done differently here. Women listened to their men. Men listened to the bishop and the elders. This was what she wanted, wasn't it? To be home again? To feel safe?

For the first time, she wondered if coming home had been the right thing to do. She had come home to be with family and friends, where she had always felt safe. But had that decision been selfish? Was she inviting danger into the lives of the people she loved? Why hadn't she considered that possibility before she'd come back?

Now it was too late. If anything happened to any-one in the community, it would be her fault.

Elizabeth looked at her mother. She should leave. Today.

But where would she go? This was her home. These people were her family. And she knew she needed their wisdom, their guidance and their love. She would tell them the truth, all of it. Then she would gauge their reactions and consider Thomas's counsel. But if she felt her presence would put her loved ones in danger she would not hesitate to leave.

"You're right, *Mamm.* I will call Thomas in for breakfast. He must be finished his chores by now."

"Gut." Mary moved to the stove and lifted a cast-iron skillet. "I cook for him every morning and he always brings a healthy appetite." Mary began fixing the meal.

"Thomas has a beard, which means he also has a wife. Doesn't his wife fix him breakfast?" She said it as nonchalantly as she could, but one glance at the smile on her mother's face and she knew she wasn't fooling anyone.

Her mother continued with her cooking and re-plied as nonchalantly. "He waited a year for you to return. Kept coming by the farm every week to see if we had heard from you. Finally, your *daed* took him aside and had a man-to-man talk with him. I don't know the details. I never asked. But

I assumed he told him to stop waiting for you because shortly afterward Thomas married."

A kaleidoscope of emotions exploded inside Elizabeth's heart. What had she expected? For him to love her forever even after she'd left him? Of course he would marry. She had been gone for *seven years*. But when she'd seen him again those years had vanished and all she saw was the man she'd once loved.

She couldn't allow those feelings to resurface. They would only cause pain. He was a married man with a family now. Besides, the reason she'd left, the secret she couldn't share with him, still existed. She'd left for his good. She'd wanted him to be happy, to marry and start a family. But she'd never realized how deeply it would hurt both of them.

Tears trickled down her cheeks. She brushed them away before her mother could see her distress.

"Did he marry someone I know?" she asked, unconsciously holding her breath, not able to picture Thomas with one of her former friends.

"He married Margaret Sue Miller. You never met her. Her family moved to Sunny Creek from Ohio a few months after you left."

Elizabeth folded her hands in her lap and pondered the information.

"I think you would have liked her," her mother said. "She was such a happy, loving woman of

Gott. She always had a smile and a kind word for everyone."

Elizabeth's head snapped up. "Was?"

"*Ja*. Poor Thomas. He lost Margaret two years ago. She died from complications during childbirth."

This new information rocked Elizabeth to her soul.

Oh, Thomas. How horrible that must have been for you.

"And the child?" Elizabeth asked.

"They had a beautiful little girl. Named her Rachel. She has a sweet disposition like her mother. She's a bundle of smiles. Not like that brother of hers. He is all boy. Skinned knees. Energy that doesn't quit. A dirt magnet, that one." Mary laughed. "I don't know how Thomas does it raising them on his own. His parents help when he is working the farm. But they leave to spend six months in Florida every winter. They left a few weeks ago. Margaret's parents help in their absence. And I step in now and then. But still the responsibility for their upbringing rests on his shoulders."

Mary carried her mug to the sink more, Elizabeth suspected, to steal a moment to collect her thoughts than to clean.

"Thomas brings the *kinner* here a couple times a month," Mary said. "He pays me to watch them while he goes into town for supplies. I think sometimes it is more to help me than to help him. He knows I love children. I am alone, and I can certainly use the little extra cash it brings. But the rest of the time he is both mother and father to those children."

"Two children?"

"*Ja.* Benjamin and Rachel."

"How old is Benjamin?"

"He just turned five."

A bittersweet smile twisted Elizabeth's lips. She was happy for Thomas. She had known years ago that he would make a good *daed* someday.

"Now, go. Get Thomas. He must be hungry by now." Mary crossed to the stove. "Tell him I have a hot breakfast waiting for him."

Elizabeth's heart fluttered. She could hardly wait to see Thomas again and yet knew she had to keep a distance between them. It wasn't just her heart that was in danger of being lost, but her life, too. She could not put Thomas at risk by being around him, especially when he had two little ones to raise. She wished she hadn't come back. She'd put her mother at risk, too, and she didn't know what to do about it. What had she been thinking? The Amish were not selfish people. They always put the community's needs before their own. Had living in the *Englisch* world changed her? Was she not Amish anymore?

She needed to rethink her situation. She couldn't

bring evil here…unless it was too late and she already had.

I will be back. Keep your mouth shut if you want to live.

A chill raced over her bones as she remembered the stranger's words.

Maybe she should go to the sheriff and tell him what she knew.

But the Amish frowned on involving outsiders in their business. They handled things together as a community whenever possible. Besides, the murder had happened in Philadelphia. What could the local sheriff do here?

How could she convince this man that she didn't know his name and wouldn't be able to identify him so she wasn't a threat? And what did he think she had? Did Hannah really tell him she'd given something to her that this man was willing to kill for? If she could talk to him, convince him she was no danger to him, maybe he would believe her and go back to Philadelphia.

The memory of his dark eyes and threatening sneer seized her breath.

Or maybe she wouldn't talk to him.

Dear Lord, how have things gone so terribly wrong? Please guide me to make good decisions. Don't let my foolishness hurt others.

Stepping outside, Elizabeth paused at the top of the porch steps and took a good look around the farm now that daylight had arrived. It was beautiful here. Peaceful. Quiet. It seemed like millions of miles away from bottleneck traffic, talking on cell phones and witnessing her best friend's murder.

But was it far enough?

She placed her fingers gently against the tender flesh of her neck. She could almost feel her attacker's grip on her throat. She knew with certainty he would return. And now, because of her selfishness, she had led an evil man straight to the doorsteps of the people she loved most.

Please help me, Lord. Please give me wisdom and guide me. I don't know what I should do now.

She stood in silence and waited.

What? Did she expect some booming voice from heaven to start telling her what to do?

What was wrong with her? She knew better. *Gott* answers all prayers. He speaks quietly in the inner recesses of one's soul. Sometimes the answer is yes, sometimes no, sometimes wait. But He answers.

She needed to learn patience and to relearn trust. Maybe He'd be slow to answer because it had been so long since He'd heard from her. For seven years she had not gone to Him for guidance, or little else for that matter. Maybe He no longer recognized her voice.

I'm sorry, Lord. Forgive me.

Placing her fears in *Gott*'s hands, she stepped into the yard and headed for the barn.

* * *

Thomas had milked the cows, put the tall metal containers of milk outside the barn for pickup for market, moved the horses into the pasture, cleaned the manure from the stalls, laid fresh straw and finished sweeping the wooden floor. There was nothing left for him to do, but he couldn't make his feet carry him to the house. Elizabeth was in the house.

A flood of emotions—anger, guilt and something else he wouldn't acknowledge—tormented him.

It was not the Amish way to hold on to anger. He'd thought he'd forgiven her. But when he saw her again, anger simmered in his blood as fresh and strong as it had the day she'd betrayed him and left.

Guilt gnawed at his insides. How could he allow himself to have any feelings of any kind for Elizabeth? Wasn't that a betrayal of his dear Margaret? He'd have to keep his distance. He wouldn't let himself betray the memory of a wife who had loved him with all her heart…like he had once loved Elizabeth.

"Thomas?"

He froze. The soft tones of her voice caressed his nerve endings like hot caramel coating an apple in autumn. His emotions tumbled and fought each other for center place. Anger won.

"Ja?" He turned to face her. He grasped the

pitchfork tightly and, barely noticing the whitening of his knuckles, tried to hide the anger flooding through his body. He knew he had failed when she glanced into his eyes and he saw guilt and sorrow looking back.

"*Mamm* wanted me to ask if you are almost finished with your chores."

He nodded. "They're done."

"*Gut.* She has a hot breakfast waiting."

"*Denki.*" He knew the word of thanks hadn't hidden the iciness in his tone but he couldn't help it. He needed time to process his feelings. Time to ask the Lord to help him forgive. Time to figure out a way to be in her presence without his heart shattering into painful shards.

She nodded and turned to leave.

"Elizabeth," he said quickly.

She froze but didn't turn back toward him.

"Who was that man? Tell me. What are you running from?"

"I'm not running from anything."

He caught her arm with his hand and turned her toward him.

"Is that what the *Englisch* taught you? To lie?"

She didn't move a muscle. She couldn't meet his eyes, either.

When she didn't answer him, he threw more questions at her.

"Why did you leave with Hannah? How could you leave your church and abandon your faith?"

"I never abandoned my faith." She kept her eyes down. "I believe today as I have always believed."

"You left your parents and your community." His voice was filled with accusation and hurt before it broke into a hoarse whisper. "You left me."

Silence beat loudly between them.

Thomas murmured a prayer for *Gott* to forgive him for harboring these negative feelings and to give him the strength he needed to forgive Elizabeth. When he spoke again, he tried to soften his tone.

"I deserved more than that handwritten note your mother gave me, which said nothing more than goodbye. *We* deserved more." He stared at her slumped shoulders and continued to wait for an answer that didn't come.

Slowly she lifted her face. "Thomas..." Her eyes pleaded for understanding but her words offered no explanation. Pain stabbed through his chest.

What had happened to his Elizabeth? Who was this stranger standing in front of him?

"Why did you *kumm* back?" He glared at her, his heart holding such hurt he could hardly bear it.

"This is my home. Where else should I be?"

He recoiled in shock as if she had slapped him. He knew his face registered his surprise but he couldn't hide his emotions. "You're staying? This is not just a visit?"

She straightened her shoulders. "I'm not sure.

When I came back, I planned to get baptized and remain here." Her voice lowered to a whisper. "Now I'm not sure that was a wise decision."

Thomas pulled her close, so only inches separated them. His breath gently fanned the loose tendrils of hair on her neck. "Why now? Why after all these years?"

She didn't answer.

He studied her closely.

"You used to be able to talk to me," he said. "We were friends…more than friends." A thread of steel laced his words. "We are not leaving this barn until you tell me the truth."

"You cannot order me around, Thomas. I am a grown woman and make my own decisions." Before he could ask any more questions, she eased her arm out of his grasp and hurried to put a distance between them. "I'll tell *Mamm* you are ready for breakfast," she called over her shoulder as she headed toward the house.

A short time later Elizabeth had just set a tray of spam, fried potatoes and scrambled eggs on the table when she heard Thomas enter the house. He joined them in the kitchen. He'd hung his hat on the rack by the front door. His face and hands were clean and water droplets glistened in his hair from cleaning up after doing his chores.

Elizabeth's pulse quickened. It was so good to see Thomas again—too good.

Thomas took a seat at the head of the table, as if he belonged there.

But why shouldn't he?

If he helped her mother every day with the heavy chores, brought his children to visit with her and then paid her besides, it was obvious he had earned that place at the table. He had done more for her mother than she had over the years, Elizabeth realized, and a wave of guilt washed over her.

"*Denki*, Mary," Thomas said as he looked at the plate of food she placed before him. "I am hungrier than I thought." He smiled at her mother and Elizabeth's heart melted with the wish that she could be the recipient of that warmth. She knew the coldness in his tone during their conversation in the barn was well-deserved. But that hadn't prevented his words from hurting her.

Elizabeth stayed silent as Thomas ate his meal. She smiled occasionally as she listened to Thomas and her *mamm* discuss the newest antics of his children, and chat about next spring's planting once the last frost had gone. She was a polite hostess as she passed plates of food and served coffee, but her mind wandered, was constantly mired in days gone by and useless musings of what-ifs.

"Elizabeth?" The surprised and stern tone in her mother's voice pulled her out of her reverie. "Thomas asked you a question."

"What?" Her gaze flew from her mother to

Thomas. "I'm sorry. My mind wandered. What did you ask, Thomas?"

"I asked about Hannah. Did the two of you remain friends after you both left our community?"

Elizabeth's heart seized. "*Ja*, we did. We were more like sisters than friends."

"How is she—" Mary asked.

"Will she be returning to Sunny Creek, too?" Thomas interrupted, his tone more accusatory than questioning. The intensity of his gaze made Elizabeth lower hers.

"No." She hoped the softness in her voice would hide the high anxiety storming through her body. Her hands trembled so she immediately folded them in her lap.

"I'm surprised," Mary said. "I know Hannah was happy here until her mother died. I always believed that one day she would return." Her mother sent her a puzzled look. "Is the *Englisch* way so appealing that it is worth leaving everything and everyone she knew behind?"

Elizabeth lightly covered her mother's hand with her own. "Hannah loved the Amish way, *Mamm*. Always. The appeal of the *Englisch* was never the reason we left. You know that."

"Then why?" An icy edge took hold in Thomas's voice.

Elizabeth and her mother gave each other a telling glance but remained silent, keeping a secret between them that neither woman was ready to share.

"It is a simple question, Elizabeth. This sister of yours, if she did not leave for love of the *Englisch*, then why isn't she returning, too?

Elizabeth squared her shoulders and met his gaze unflinchingly. She saw the anger, pain and confusion in his eyes, and she felt sorry for him. His question wasn't about Hannah. It was about them and her betrayal. Yes, she owed him an explanation. But not now. Not yet. The time wasn't right. She wondered if the time would ever be right. She offered him a gentle smile and spoke softly. "As I said, Thomas. Hannah won't be returning home."

"Then she couldn't have loved our way of life as much as you say," he said.

"Leaving Sunny Creek was one of the hardest things Hannah ever did."

"Couldn't have been too hard. She left. You both did."

Elizabeth remained silent beneath the verbal slap of his tone. She knew it was pain speaking.

Mary stood and gathered up some of the empty platters. "What does it matter now, Thomas? It happened so many years ago. Elizabeth has *kumm* home. Let us be happy about that."

"I am sorry if I upset you, Mary. But I am confused." Again he turned his focus on Elizabeth. "Why is asking a simple question so difficult to answer? If Hannah loved it here as much as you say, if you are as close as sisters, then why hasn't Hannah returned with you?"

"Because Hannah's dead."

Mary gasped. "What? Hannah died?" She placed the platters back onto the table and sank down into her chair.

Elizabeth's words caused a heavy silence to descend on the room for several seconds.

Thomas, appearing surprised and chagrined, spoke more softly. "I am sorry you lost your friend. That must have been very difficult for you."

"She was so young," Mary said. "You never told me she was ill. I would have told you to bring her home. I would have helped care for her. When did this happen?"

Elizabeth knew she'd have to tell them the details. She should have told her mother last night, when she showed up on her doorstep unannounced. But she'd played mind games with herself, pretending that if she didn't say the words out loud then they wouldn't be true.

She folded her hands together again and braced herself. "Hannah wasn't ill, *Mamm*. She was murdered."

Neither Mary nor Thomas spoke, they simply glanced at each other then back at Elizabeth and waited.

Her thoughts did a somersault through her

mind. How much should she tell them? How much was their right to know versus her desire to dump this heavy burden on other shoulders, too? With every passing second she was certain it had been selfish to come home and bring a potential danger with her. What had she been thinking?

She hadn't been thinking. She'd simply known the Amish community always took care of their own, and her love of that community, her need for their guidance and their help, had brought her home.

"Tell us what happened." Thomas's calm tone soothed her. His strength gave her courage.

"Hannah and I had just rented a condo together. I was helping move some of her things. I came in the back door and—and..."

Mary reached over and clasped Elizabeth's hand.

Elizabeth glanced back and forth between her mother and Thomas. She only saw empathy and kindness looking back. She inhaled deeply then continued the story. "I saw Hannah lying motionless on the floor of the kitchen. A man was bent over her, his hands around her throat."

Mary cried out and offered a quick prayer.

"Go on, Elizabeth." Thomas's entire demeanor offered her encouragement and strength.

"I screamed when I saw what was happening. The man stood up and raced toward me. I turned and ran as fast as I could. He almost caught up with me but I got away."

"How?" Mary asked.

"I learned how to drive while I was gone, *Mamm*. I jumped in my car and drove away."

"And Hannah?" Mary asked.

"I called the police and then doubled back to the complex. Shortly after I got back, I saw them carry her body out on a gurney to the coroner's van. There was nothing more I could do for her so…" She threw a glance between them. "I came home."

Mary got up and threw her arms around her daughter. "As you should have." She tilted Elizabeth's chin to look at her. "Why didn't you tell me?"

"I should have," Elizabeth replied. "I'm sorry, *Mamm*."

"Now I understand." Thomas's voice caught both women's attention. "The man who attacked you in the barn. He murdered Hannah and he followed you here."

Elizabeth nodded.

Mary gasped again. "Is that who you were looking out the window for this morning?"

Elizabeth hugged her mother tightly. "I'm sorry. I wasn't thinking. I never should have come home."

"Nonsense."

"You don't understand, *Mamm*. I have brought

danger home to you, to this community." Elizabeth sprang to her feet. "I need to leave."

Mary caught her hand and stopped her. "Leave? Where would you go? What would you do? You cannot face this terrible thing alone."

"Mary is right." Thomas gestured to the seat Elizabeth had vacated. "Sit. Have another cup of coffee. We'll talk and together we'll decide what the right thing is to do."

"Thomas." Elizabeth's eyes pooled with tears. "The man knows I can identify him. He can't afford to let me get away."

"What do you think he will do?" Mary asked. "Do you think he will try to kill you, again?"

"Ja, Mamm." Elizabeth lowered herself back into her chair. "And anyone else who tries to help me. That's why I have to go. I was wrong to come and it would be wrong to stay."

"It is wrong to leave." The iron steeliness crept back into Thomas's voice. "Running is not the answer to problems. I would have hoped you'd have learned that lesson by now."

A heated flush painted her cheeks. She knew his words had a double meaning. She hadn't run away before. She had chosen to leave. For him. For his happiness. But she knew he couldn't know that.

"I won't be able to live with myself if anyone gets hurt because of me." Her eyes pleaded with him to understand.

"No one will get hurt. The Amish community takes care of its own and you are still one of us, Elizabeth. We will talk to the bishop and ask his guidance. Everything will be all right."

"Thomas is right. The bishop will have sound advice." Mary sat down again. "Don't worry. *Gott* will protect us."

"He didn't protect Hannah." Elizabeth regretted the words the moment they left her lips.

"You must not question *Gott*," Mary said, reprimanding her. "It was His will that Hannah be called home. And we must place this problem in His hands. He loves us. He has a plan for our lives. Whatever happens it will be His will. Trust Him, Elizabeth, always."

She lowered her eyes in chagrin. "I do, *Mamm*. I shouldn't have said that. I'm sorry."

"Finish your coffee." Thomas gestured to her mug. "Tell us everything. We will make a plan to keep you safe." Thomas's resolve remained solid and steady.

Elizabeth dared to relax a moment, to allow someone else to help her carry the burden. The ghost of a smile crossed her lips as she looked at Thomas. He had always been there for her. He was there for her now. But she couldn't miss his thundercloud expression as he said one more thing.

"This plan, Elizabeth, will not include running away."

THREE

Elizabeth moved quickly through the barn toward the rear exit.

"Where are you going?" Thomas stepped out of the shadows.

She startled and spun in his direction. "Don't creep up on me. You're going to give me a heart attack."

"You're too young for a heart attack. And I'm not the one who appears to be creeping around."

"Don't be foolish. I'm not creeping anywhere."

"I thought you'd be in the kitchen helping Mary clean up," Thomas said.

"And I thought you'd left for home."

"I was leaving." He came closer. "But I remembered one of the horses has a sore on his leg and I wanted to take a second look at it." He grinned. "Your turn. What are you doing scampering through the barn?"

"I don't scamper."

He raised an eyebrow and grinned. The Elizabeth he had known all his life never walked if she could avoid it. She scampered, scurried, skipped and frolicked through life. It did his heart good to see that some things about her hadn't changed.

"I was going to check on my car." She waved her hand toward the rear barn doors. "I've got it under a tarp behind the barn."

"And you think one of the livestock took it for a joyride?"

Elizabeth laughed at his foolishness, which was exactly what he wanted. He'd always tried to make her happy and her life carefree. He knew she needed a heavy dose of that now. Besides, he had always loved to hear the tinkling sound of her giggles and was not disappointed to hear them now.

"That is a ridiculous notion and you know it." But she covered her mouth to stop a giggle anyway and he smiled. "If I am going to stay, I have to get the car shipshape and ready to sell."

"If you stay?" he asked.

"We haven't spoken to the bishop yet. He might not want me to stay."

Thomas grinned. He didn't speak but sent her a knowing glance.

"Okay. So he's probably going to let me stay. But I'll still have to sell my car."

"How did it feel to be able to drive your own car?"

"I must admit that is one of the *Englisch* luxuries I really enjoyed."

"Will you miss it?"

"Nah. If I feel like driving, I'll climb on one of the plows and take a spin in the fields with the horses."

Now Thomas had to laugh, as his mind painted a picture of that event.

"I find it hard to picture you behind the wheel of a car," he said. "You seem more the buggy type."

"I am the buggy type. Always have been. But I loved my little Honda Fit, with its racing stripes on the side."

"Honda Fit?"

"Yep. C'mon. I'll show it to you."

Like a flash she was off, scampering across the barn floor toward the back exit. Thomas chuckled, pushed off from the stall he'd been leaning against and lumbered after her.

"Thomas."

The urgency in her voice made his blood run cold. What if that man had returned? He raced toward the back of the barn. When he cleared the open doorway, he skidded to a stop.

Elizabeth stood to his right, leaning heavily against the barn wall.

Thomas shot a hurried glance in every other direction, trying to find the danger or intruder, but saw nothing. His eyes moved back toward Elizabeth and his heart squeezed. She looked so fragile and small and scared. Her body trembled and the piece of paper she held in her hand rattled.

"Elizabeth? What's wrong?"

The blood had drained from her face. She was almost as white as the paper she held in her hands. Fear widened her eyes and she didn't speak. Shakily, she held out the note.

He slid it from her fingers. Anger coursed through his body when he read the words:

I want what is mine. I will contact you again soon with a time and place to meet. Tell no one. I warn you, give it to me or die.

"*Kumm* in. Sit down." Bishop Eli Schwartz ushered Thomas, Elizabeth and Mary into the front room. His wife, Sarah, offered them tea and cookies, which they gratefully accepted. Once his wife had left the room, the bishop turned his attention to his guests.

"Welcome back, Elizabeth. It is good to see you again. I heard you were back. Are you here for a visit or are you planning to stay?"

Elizabeth wasn't surprised he had heard she was back. Nothing traveled faster in the Amish community than news. She tried unsuccessfully not to squirm in her seat. Instead she attempted to hide her nervousness by clasping her fingers tightly in her lap.

"My intention, Bishop, was to be baptized and move back permanently."

"Wonderful." The bishop's gaze flew from one to the other before it settled on Elizabeth. He raised a brow. "And now?"

Thomas glanced at her for permission and when she nodded he took over the conversation. She listened with only half an ear as he filled in the bishop on everything that had happened in the past twenty-four hours.

She released a breath and relaxed. She knew she shouldn't be relying on Thomas. She should be explaining the circumstances to the bishop on her own. She was strong, independent and hadn't needed a man's help for seven years. She didn't need a man to speak for her now.

But having someone to talk to, someone to comfort her, someone to make her feel protected and safe, even if just for a little while—was that really so bad?

"Elizabeth?"

She startled at the sound of her name.

"The piece of paper?" The bishop held out his hand.

Elizabeth drew the folded paper from her apron pocket and handed it over.

The older man studied it, deep furrows appearing in his forehead and at the sides of his mouth. Then he folded the paper and handed it back to her.

"Who else knows about this?" he asked.

"No one."

The bishop nodded, leaned back in his chair and silently stroked his beard.

"I am willing to leave, Bishop, if you think it would be best for everyone else," Elizabeth said.

"I am sure *Gott* has waited patiently for you to return, to repent and be baptized." The bishop smiled, sipped his tea and then placed the cup back down on the side table. "I know your *mamm* has waited many years for you to find your way home. Now you are here. That is a *gut* thing. Who am I to send you away?"

"But this man?"

"We will deal with him. I will speak with the elders and tell them what is going on. Meanwhile, you need to go home. Keep your eyes open. Don't go anywhere alone. Don't do anything foolish."

"Should we tell the sheriff?" Thomas asked.

Elizabeth knew it was hard for him to ask that question of the bishop because the Amish do not like to involve the *Englisch*, especially law enforcement, in their lives.

"I don't think that is necessary yet." The bishop nodded toward Elizabeth's pocket, which housed the note. "The man wants to meet with Elizabeth. Until he contacts her again, I do not believe she is in any immediate danger." He stroked his beard again. "What do you have that he wants? What did Hannah give you?"

"She didn't give me anything. I don't know what this man wants." Elizabeth tried to remember every conversation between them on the day of Hannah's death.

"Wait!" She leaned forward. "I have a carton of Hannah's belongings. I dropped the one I was carrying into the condo when I ran for my life, but I had another one still in my car." She couldn't keep the excitement and hope out of her voice. "That must be it! Whatever the man wants must be in that box."

"Where is this box?" the bishop asked.

"On the floor of the backseat of my car." She shot a hurried glance at each one of them. "I completely forgot about it. It has to be in the box. I don't have anything else."

"Gut." The bishop's lips twisted in a wry grin. "For now, we will play his game. We will let him think we are willing to return this elusive item. No sheriff. Not yet. Let me discuss it with the elders first. You go home and search through that box. Whatever was worth killing poor Hannah over should be easy to recognize. When we know what we are dealing with we will decide the proper way to proceed."

The bishop stood, indicating the meeting was over. Thomas, Elizabeth and Mary stood, as well.

"Denki, Bishop Schwartz, for seeing us without notice. We appreciate it," Thomas said. He placed a hand under Elizabeth's elbow. "I will do my best

to keep an eye on things at the farm the best I can and I will try to keep Elizabeth and Mary safe."

"Gut." The bishop nodded. "I will speak with the others and get back with you shortly. Elizabeth, if there are any problems, ring the porch triangle and we will all *kumm* running."

Elizabeth smiled and nodded. "Thank you, Bishop."

"Meanwhile, stay safe. Go about your business. Prepare for your repentance and baptism. Let us pray about what the next move should be. And let me know immediately if there are any more letters."

"Denki. I feel better already."

Thomas helped both women into the buggy, then went around to the other side. After nodding goodbye to the bishop, he clicked the reins and guided the horse back toward the main road.

"See, Elizabeth," Mary said. "The bishop will know what to do. Everything will be all right."

They'd traveled about a quarter of a mile when Thomas spoke. "I thought the meeting went well. I told you the bishop would not ask you to leave."

"It's not that. I knew Bishop Schwartz would allow me to stay. He has known me and my family since I was born."

"Then what is it?"

"The danger is real, Thomas. I am not afraid for myself, but what have I brought to the community?"

Thomas placed his hand over hers. A pleasant

tingling sensation raced up her arms. Even now, she could still be affected by the mere touch of his hand.

"We will keep you safe, Elizabeth. The whole community will be watching for strangers and things that are out of place."

"I know." A pounding headache formed in the sinus area above her eyes. "But what if it isn't enough? What if he hurts someone?"

"Maybe we will find what he wants in that box in your car. We will give it to him and he will go back to Philadelphia."

"Do you really believe he will take the box and leave?"

"If he wanted you dead, he had the few extra minutes to do it in the barn before I could reach you."

Elizabeth felt the blood drain from her face as she realized the truth of his words. He could have killed her in the barn. Almost did. But a sense of dread filled her. What if he was lying? What if he had no intention of letting her live once he'd gotten what he came for? She'd seen his face. She was a witness to his crime. She'd lived in the *Englisch* world long enough to know criminals didn't leave witnesses behind.

"What you have is more important to him right now than you dead."

The truth of his words gave her a little inner peace.

"What do you think Hannah put in the box?" he asked.

"That's just it, Thomas, I don't know. And I'm scared to death to find out."

The steady clopping of the horse's hooves was the only sound for several more miles as Thomas pondered the day's events. He'd make sure Elizabeth and Mary were settled in and then he'd have to head home. His former in-laws would be bringing the *kinner* home soon.

A smile bowed his lips at the mental image of his two precious children. *Gott* had blessed him with two precious gifts—his smile widened— even if one of those gifts was perpetually drawn to dirt and mire.

His smile didn't last. How was he going to keep Elizabeth and Mary safe when he was miles away on his own farm?

He couldn't and that was unacceptable. He had to find a way to protect them daily. But how?

"You're awfully quiet, Thomas. Is something wrong?" Elizabeth studied him closely.

Something wrong? Everything's wrong.

When he woke this morning his only thought was getting his chores finished for Mary in time to get back home to take care of his own farm and his *kinner*. He'd never expected his world to be turned upside down. But the unexpected events in this life reminded him that he was not in control, *Gott* was.

"Nothing's wrong, Elizabeth. Just thinking through the day's events," Thomas replied.

When Elizabeth smiled at him, his heart skipped a beat. After all these years she could still stir deep feelings in him and, for a moment, he hated himself for that weakness.

"It's been a crazy day," she admitted.

"Ja."

"Denki, Thomas."

He glanced her way and for an instant was lost in the sky-blue depths of her eyes.

"I know you weren't expecting to see me," she said. "And...well, I am grateful for all you have done. Helping my mother on the farm. Taking me to see the bishop. You didn't have to do any of it and I want you to know I appreciate it."

Thomas nodded. "Many things have passed between us, Elizabeth, and many years. But not so many that we can't consider each other a friend."

Did her smile dim when he called her a friend? Was it possible she harbored deeper feelings, too? No. His mind played games with his hopes. If she'd cared for him as he'd cared for her, she would never have left.

She twisted her hands in her lap and gazed off in the distance.

"Elizabeth?"

She sighed deeply. "I'm sorry. I can't stop thinking about the note."

"The note is keeping you safe," Mary said. "It's giving you time to find out what this mystery item is. There is nothing to worry about. *Gott* will protect us."

"Mary's right," Thomas said. "I'd say the man got what he wanted for now. He frightened you. He put you on edge. He has you looking over your shoulder at every shadow and jumping at every sound."

Thomas clicked the reins and the horse broke into a trot as their buggy turned onto the dirt path leading to the house.

"This will be over soon, Elizabeth," Thomas assured her. "The first thing we need to do is search the box." He pulled the buggy in front of the porch and helped both women down. Mary climbed the steps to the house, while Elizabeth almost ran toward the barn.

Thomas tied the reins to the porch railing then walked toward the barn, where Elizabeth had disappeared only moments before. Could the words he'd offered her for comfort turn out true? Would it be that easy? Give the man what he wants and he'll leave them alone? What could be so important it was worth killing an innocent woman to get? His curiosity grew with each step as he neared the barn.

Mary cried out. "Thomas. Elizabeth. *Kumm* quickly."

Thomas spun back toward the house and ran. He burst inside. The older woman was pressed against the wall, her knees nearly buckling.

"Mary?"

"Mamm?" Elizabeth whooshed through the doorway and came up short behind him. "Are you all right? What's wrong?"

Mary lifted a trembling hand and pointed.

"Oh, no!" Elizabeth whispered as both of them looked in the direction Mary had indicated.

The house had been ransacked. The cushions of the sofa and chairs had been gutted with something sharp and stuffing covered every surface. The end tables were overturned, some broken.

The destruction spilled into the kitchen. Every cabinet door hung open. Every drawer was pulled out and emptied. Silverware and cooking utensils had been carelessly tossed across the linoleum. Canisters of flour and sugar were emptied onto the floor. Pots and pans had been thrown haphazardly into the messy concoction.

Every nook and cranny had been searched, every chance to destroy something had been taken.

"He was here," Mary whispered. "That evil man was in our home."

Elizabeth rushed to her mother's side and wrapped her arms around her. "It's okay, *Mamm*. We're okay. We aren't hurt. This is just stuff. We can fix stuff, right?"

Mary nodded, a stunned expression still deeply etched on her face.

Although Thomas knew Elizabeth was doing her best to comfort her mother and ease her fears, she couldn't hide the tremor in her own voice from him. He knew her too well. She was terrified.

Both women looked at the destruction surrounding them and remained speechless.

Suddenly Mary headed toward the stairs. "He must have gone upstairs, too."

Thomas stopped her before she could reach the bottom step. "I will *kumm* back and take care of whatever damage was done. Right now we have to leave."

"Leave?" Elizabeth threw him a questioning glance. "Where will we go?"

"Home. With me." Thomas shot Elizabeth a look that let her know he would not take no for an answer. "But not before we retrieve that box and take it with us. It's time to see what is so important inside."

FOUR

Elizabeth couldn't stop tapping her toe or fumbling with her fingers in her lap. The steady sound of the horse's hooves clomping up the lane did little to calm her frayed nerves.

"It will be all right, Elizabeth." Thomas smiled and she assumed he was trying to reassure her. "That man does not know where you are going. You and Mary will be safe with me."

If he only knew. The stranger wasn't what made her pulse race and her body tremble with nervous energy. It was seeing his family home, meeting his children. Witnessing a life she'd always wanted but couldn't allow herself to hope for.

"I'm not afraid, Thomas. I know you will do your best to protect us."

The buggy turned onto a dirt lane between two white picket fences and her heart stuttered. She could see a two-story white clapboard house in the distance, with a large front porch. Two adults sat in rocking chairs watching a young boy run around the yard. She saw all of them turn their way as the buggy approached.

"Whoa." Thomas stopped the buggy at the edge of the porch, then leaped out and reached up a hand to help Mary down from the back seat.

Elizabeth stepped down and came around the buggy just in time to see a towheaded boy barrel across the yard and fling himself at Thomas.

"*Daed—Daed, kumm* here. Hurry. I found a little cat hiding in the barn. Can I keep him? *Kumm* see." The boy tugged on his father's hand.

"Benjamin, mind your manners. We have company." He tousled his son's hair. "Say hello. We can go to look at the cat in a little while."

The boy peered around his father and seemed surprised to see Elizabeth. His enthusiasm for the cat was tempered and he peered at her with the cutest look of curiosity on his face.

"Who are you?" He let go of his *daed*'s hand and came closer to her. "I don't know you. Where did you come from?"

"Benjamin. Manners." His father's warning tone caused the boy to lower his eyes and stop talking.

"It's okay," Elizabeth assured Thomas. She squatted down to be eye level with the child. When he looked into her face, her heart seized. He was the spitting image of his father. "Hello, Benjamin. My name is Elizabeth. I am Mary's daughter and I am a friend of your *daed*'s."

The boy's eyes grew wide. He glanced at Mary and then back to her. "I didn't know Miss Mary could have old *kinners*. I thought all *kinners* were little like me."

Elizabeth laughed. "Little *kinners* grow up. You will, too, someday." She offered him her hand. She grinned as he placed his little fingers in her grasp and shook her hand. "Nice to meet you, Benjamin."

He took back his hand. "Do you like cats?"

Elizabeth stood and smiled down at the boy. "I do like cats. When I was little like you, my *daed* let me keep a whole family of kittens in our barn. When they grew up to be adult cats they earned their keep by keeping the field mice away from the barn."

Benjamin grinned and grabbed her hand. "*Kumm* with me. There's a cat in our barn. I'll show you."

"Benjamin, what did I say?" Thomas placed his hands on his son's shoulders. "There will be time for that later, *sohn*. Miss Mary and Miss Elizabeth have things to do right now. You go play in the barn with your cat. We will join you soon."

Benjamin didn't need any extra urging. He was off in a flash, running across the yard toward the barn.

"He's adorable." Elizabeth smiled at Thomas and the look of pride in his eyes made her heart swell.

"*Kumm*." He placed a hand on her elbow. "Meet the rest of my family."

Mary had already gone up on the porch and was in deep conversation with the two people sitting there. As Elizabeth climbed the stairs, they stood. The man welcomed her first.

"*Gut* afternoon. My name is Isaac. I am sorry to hear of your troubles." He looped his fingers in his suspenders and moved to the side. "This is my wife, Rebecca."

"Hello." The woman stepped forward. "Welcome." She held a toddler in her arms, and she was one of the most beautiful little girls Elizabeth had ever seen. The child sucked on her index finger and stared at her with stunningly blue eyes. Thomas's eyes.

Elizabeth's eyes burned with tears and she fought hard not to shed them.

This is Thomas's family. This is what I had always wanted for him. So why, Lord, does it hurt so much?

"Hello, little one." She smiled and clasped the child's free fingers. "You must be Rachel."

"*Ja.* This is my precious one." Thomas took her from Rebecca's arms. The child giggled in his arms and pulled at his beard. Absently, he placed a kiss on her forehead.

Elizabeth's insides melted as she watched. He was a good *daed*. She knew he would be.

"Let's go inside. I started a fresh pot of coffee. It should be ready by now," Rebecca said. She looked at the two women. "Dinner will be ready shortly. There is plenty of food. You are welcome to join us."

"*Ja*, thank you, Rebecca. Mary and Elizabeth will be joining us for all meals for a while. I have invited them to stay in the *dawdi haus* for a short time. You and Isaac are no longer needing it now that you've bought a farm of your own. My parents stay in the main house with me six months out of the year. It was built for family. Seems foolish to let it stand empty. Mary and Elizabeth need a place to stay so I am offering it to them."

A surprised expression flashed across Rebecca's face, but she covered her reaction quickly. She smiled at the two women. "Both of you are welcome." She reached out her arms to Thomas for Rachel. "*Kumm*. I will set out mugs for us.

Thomas handed his daughter back to her. "*Ja*. We have much to discuss." He turned to his guests. "Right after dinner I will show you to the *dawdi haus*. Usually there is a connecting door and a small bedroom in these in-law apartments but I actually had a small house added on to my own. There is a connecting door off the kitchen. But you will also find a living room, two bedrooms, a kitchen and a bathroom inside. Now that Isaac and Rebecca have chosen to purchase their own farm, it is sitting empty. You are both welcome to use it for as long as you need."

"*Denki*, Thomas. We are grateful for the help." Mary put her arms around Elizabeth's waist and steered her toward the kitchen. Without a word passing between them, Elizabeth knew her *mamm* understood how awkward and difficult meeting Thomas's family was for her. Her mother's secure touch around her waist let Elizabeth know she wasn't going through any of it alone. Again, her eyes burned with threatening tears. She had missed her *mamm*…so much.

"I will bring in your bags from the buggy and, of course, the box. I am anxious to see what great secret is inside." Thomas bounded down the porch steps before anyone could reply.

Thomas had done most of the talking as he brought his in-laws up-to-date on the day's events. Even as he spoke he had to admit being surprised with how much had transpired in only a day's time. He wasn't surprised, however, at their kindness toward Elizabeth, or their sincere desire to help in any way they could. They were good people and he was honored to have them as family.

Crash!

Finishing his second cup of coffee, Thomas pushed it aside, jumped to his feet and ran in the direction of the trouble, closely followed by the rest of the adults.

Benjamin stood in the middle of the room. He had overturned the box Thomas had placed on the sofa and its contents had scattered across the wooden floor. Benjamin's lips puckered and his eyes welled with tears as if he might cry at any moment. "I'm sorry, *Daed*. Don't be mad at me. It was an accident."

"I am not mad, *sohn*. But you know better than to touch things that do not belong to you."

Everyone helped to pick up the strewn items. There were half a dozen books, a couple of plants, a set of sheets, some bath towels, a few knick-knacks and even a few small framed pictures.

Thomas held one photo in his hand and stared at it. "This is a picture of Hannah. The Amish do not take pictures of themselves. Maybe Hannah became more *Englisch* than you thought in the years you were gone."

"That is one vice Hannah did like," Elizabeth said. "She took pictures. Lots of them. She wanted to have something besides her mind to record her memories. I think she felt it was concrete proof that she belonged somewhere with people she cared about and who cared about her, after feeling for so many years that she didn't."

"And you?" Thomas asked as he handed the small picture frame to Elizabeth. "Did you take pictures of yourself, too?"

"Not really." Elizabeth took the frame from his hand, looked at it and smiled at the image of her friend. "Hannah snapped one or two of me over the years when I was doing something with her group of friends." She shrugged. "But it was different for me. I always knew who I was and where I came from. I did not need reminders."

One by one, the adults handed various items to Elizabeth as she repacked the carton.

Once most of the items had been cleaned up, Mary and Rebecca returned to the kitchen to finish getting dinner ready and Isaac excused himself to tend to the animals in the barn, leaving the children with Thomas and Elizabeth.

"I'm sure Benjamin meant no harm, Thomas." She kneeled down so she could be on eye level with the upset child. "You were probably curious, weren't you? Wondering what I had in the box."

The boy nodded.

"Why don't you help me pick up the few things that are left and put them back in the box? Can you do that?"

Benjamin nodded and grinned. He picked up a few things and threw them into the carton.

Thomas eyed every item going back into the box. A key chain. More pictures. Even a small stuffed rabbit. When there were no items left on the floor for the boy to retrieve, he patted his son's rump. "Go, Benjamin. Get washed up for dinner."

The boy scampered off.

"I don't understand." Thomas placed the last item he'd been holding in his hand on the top of the carton. "I don't see anything unusual. Certainly nothing worth harming someone to get back."

Elizabeth sat back on her heels. "I know. I was

thinking the same thing. I can't imagine what that man thinks is so important." She picked up two of the books and briefly leafed through their pages. "No notes tucked inside." She rummaged through the box, making sure she hadn't missed something. "And no journals or anything else that would expose this man's identity."

"We must be missing something."

"Maybe the missing item was inside the box I dropped at the condo."

Thomas shook his head. "I am sure the man searched that box before he came all this way." He reached out a hand and helped Elizabeth to her feet. "I've been wondering about that, too. Are you sure you don't remember seeing him before? How would he even begin to know where you might have gone? It doesn't make sense that he would show up on an Amish farm looking for you. I thought you and Hannah had given up the Amish life. Why would he think of looking for you here?"

"We had. No one knew of our past."

"You are wrong, Elizabeth. This man knew."

"Hannah must have told him. But I don't know why she would do such a thing." Elizabeth sighed heavily. "There are many things I don't understand. Hannah and I were best friends. I didn't think we kept secrets from each other."

Thomas saw great sadness in her eyes when she looked at him. "I wish she hadn't kept this man a secret. Maybe I could have helped her. Maybe she wouldn't have been murdered."

Thomas frowned. "There has to be something here. What about the pictures? Anything special? Is the man in any of them?"

Elizabeth took a second look. "No. They are photos of friends Hannah made at the restaurant where she worked." She held one in particular in her hand. "She had just started dating this young man." Elizabeth showed Thomas a photo of Hannah and a young *Englisch* man, their heads together, eating cotton candy at a fair and grinning into the camera. "I hadn't met him yet. She'd only gone out with him a few times. But she spoke well of him. I think she was starting to really like him." Her expression clouded. "I wonder if anyone told him about her death. The police, maybe?"

Thomas handed her back the picture. "I am sorry, Elizabeth. I know it must pain you to have lost your friend."

Elizabeth remained silent, lost in her own thoughts, but grief was etched in her features. She startled him when she suddenly darted across the room. "No, honey. Don't put that in your mouth."

Rachel, sitting on the floor next to a bookshelf, had something in her hands headed directly for her mouth. She'd been so quiet the adults had overlooked her.

Thomas quickly reached his daughter and took the item from the child's hands, and her cries instantly filled the room. "What is this?" He held up a small plastic white dog with black spots on its back and wearing a red collar.

Elizabeth glanced at it and laughed. "It's a toy dog from a popular comic strip. Hannah loved this character. She had pictures, a key ring, even a stuffed animal just like this."

Rachel's wailing continued. She stood up and pulled on her father's pant leg. "Doggy." Rachel held out her hand for the toy.

"Can I give it back to her?" Elizabeth asked. "It's too large for her to swallow and there are no rough edges. She can't get hurt. It's simply a plastic toy. A decoration for Hannah's desk or bookshelf. She collected them all the time."

"If you think it best." Thomas handed the small plastic toy to Elizabeth and watched as she bent down to offer it to his daughter. His breath caught in his throat at the tenderness in her expression. Once, many years ago, he had imagined Elizabeth softly mothering a house full of *kinner*, his *kinner*. Now she was here. In his living room, with his daughter—his and Margaret's daughter—and a wave of guilt washed over him.

What's the matter with me? I shouldn't be thinking about days past, about dreams long gone. I shouldn't be thinking of any other woman and sullying Margaret's memory.

Feeling angry and confused, he tried to distract himself. "Let me move the bookcase. Maybe something else rolled under it." Thomas pulled the wood case out from the wall but found nothing.

The youngster, content with having the plastic dog returned, banged it up and down on the floor and made woofing sounds as she played.

Elizabeth straightened and silently watched the child. She wrapped her arms around her body. Her worried expression concerned him.

"Are you *allrecht*?"

"Yes, I'm fine." She faced him, her troubled expression evident. "What should we do, Thomas? I can't find anything in the box of any importance. Certainly nothing significant enough to cost Hannah her life. I don't think we have what this man wants."

"We will deliver the box and its contents to him."

Her eyes widened. "I don't understand. You told us we would be safe here. How will he find us? He couldn't know I would come here."

"We will find him."

Elizabeth's mouth formed a perfect *O*. "Find *him*? How?"

"I left a note on your mother's door before we left. I told him I was taking you and your mother to a safe place but I promised him I would bring the box to the house tomorrow morning. If all goes well, he will *kumm* back to the house, read the note and wait."

"Did you sign it?"

"Of course not, Elizabeth. That would have defeated the purpose of bringing you here to keep you safe."

Elizabeth nodded. "You're right. I'm not thinking clearly."

Thomas grinned. "We know. That is why you have a whole community working together to keep you and your mother safe."

His words did little to soothe her. She looked more worried than ever.

"What if we don't have what he wants?"

He raised an eyebrow. "I have heard many what-ifs from you. You never used to question things so much before."

"I never witnessed my best friend get murdered or found myself running for my life before, either." She wrapped her arms tighter, as if she had felt a chill. "Seriously, Thomas, what if we don't have what he wants?"

"Hopefully, even if what he wants is not inside the box, he will believe you don't have it and he will go away."

Her eyes darkened. "And if he doesn't go away?"

"We will cross that bridge when we *kumm* to it. No sense worrying. We cannot change what is. Trust in the Lord. He will guide us on the right path."

Elizabeth didn't respond right away. She sat on the sofa and pretended to be watching Rachel play on the floor. But Thomas knew her too well. He could see she was thinking hard about the situation. He knew she was determined not to bring harm to him or his family or anyone in the community if she could help it. He offered a silent prayer that her solution wouldn't be to run away like she had seven years ago.

Finally, she glanced up at him.

"I will do as you say, Thomas. For now."

FIVE

Elizabeth held up her lantern. "Thomas? Is that you?" She moved closer to the porch steps and held her lantern higher.

Thomas heard the fear in her voice and hurried to reassure her. "*Ja*, it's me." He knew she was thinking about the stranger who had stepped out of the darkness and wrapped his hands around her throat.

"*Guder mariye*, Elizabeth. I'm sorry if I startled you."

"Good morning to you, too. You didn't scare me. I am scaring myself, Thomas, with foolish thoughts."

But her thoughts were far from foolish. Lord, thank You for keeping her safe. Thank You for putting me in the right place at the right time to help. Grant me the wisdom and strength to continue to keep them safe.

Thomas, leading his mare out of the barn and approaching the buggy already parked in front of the house, stopped at the bottom of the porch steps. "Did you and Mary sleep well?"

"*Ja*, we did. *Denki*. It is a fine house, Thomas. We are very comfortable. I am grateful for your kindness." She came down the few steps from the *dawdi haus* and stood beside him as he fastened the horse in place.

"Where are you going so early?"

"I am leaving for your mother's farm. The cows need milking and the stalls will not clean themselves."

"Of course, how could I forget? You go there every morning." She glanced over her shoulder toward the house. "Wait for me. I'll tell *Mamm* and go with you."

Fear no longer laced her words. She actually sounded a little happy, maybe even excited to be joining him.

"What? No." He shook his head. "You are not going with me."

She planted her hands on her hips.

Uh-oh. He couldn't miss the glare she shot his way even with only the light from the lantern illuminating the darkness. He recognized that stance. He'd seen it several times when they were younger. She'd dig in her heels like a mule not wanting to move to pasture. He released a heavy sigh. He knew there would be a battle ahead. What a way to start his day! Maybe he should have tried to sneak away earlier.

"You are not going to the farm without me, Thomas. I am home now. It is my responsibility to help my mother take care of her livestock and her farm."

"It is a man's work. You can stay and prepare a *gut* breakfast for me. I will have worked up an appetite by the time I *kumm* home."

She bristled at his words. "I can't believe you just said that to me. I am perfectly capable of cleaning out stalls, laying hay and milking cows. Maybe you should stay here and fix breakfast for *me*. That is, if you know how to cook at all."

Thomas chuckled under his breath. Yep, this is the Elizabeth he knew. Fiercely independent. Always demanding to be treated as an equal. Wanting to be a partner in every endeavor and more times than not getting her way because no one had the energy necessary to oppose her and win.

"Ahh, I was wondering if the old you still existed. You never did like being told what to do. I've been surprised you've been as cooperative as you've been."

"I've matured. I don't get as upset as I did when I was younger at the foolishness of men's words. And I've been grateful for your help and your kindness. But don't confuse gratitude with weakness, Thomas. I am capable of doing many things, not just cooking."

He finished harnessing the mare and acted like he hadn't heard a word she said. "You will be safe here. I will not be more than a few hours." He put his foot on the buggy step and hoisted himself up to the bench seat.

Elizabeth held the lantern closer. The light illuminated the carton tucked neatly behind on the floor. "You are taking the box with you. You are hoping to give it to that horrible man."

He didn't reply. He knew she wouldn't listen to reason. He reached for the reins.

Elizabeth hurried in front of the horse, grabbed the bit and blocked the path forward. "You must not do this thing alone, Thomas. I will not let you."

He raised an eyebrow. "You will not *let* me?"

"This man killed Hannah. He can kill you, too. You have *kinner*. Think of them. Speaking of which, where are the *kinner* now?"

"Isaac picked them up about a half hour ago as he does every morning."

"Okay. Fine, then." She glanced over her shoulder toward the house and then back to the buggy.

He tried to hide the grin pulling at the corners of his mouth. She wanted to tell Mary where she was going, but she didn't trust him to stay where he was when she ran inside. The indecision was killing her and he had to admit he found the whole situation funny. She'd already won. He had always given in to her if she wanted something badly enough. Only once had he ever told her no. Only once had he refused to accept her decision. Yet, she'd left anyway.

Elizabeth could be a formidable force when she wanted to be. It was one of the things that aggravated him the most and also one of the many things that he admired and drew him to her. Such strength! Like watching dark clouds gathering on the horizon and knowing you could not stop the storm.

"Let me run and tell *Mamm* where I am going. I will be right back. Do not leave without me, Thomas. If you do, I will follow on my own."

"Why are you doing this? You think you can keep me safe?" He chuckled. "Really? It wasn't me who was being choked in the barn yesterday."

Elizabeth chewed on her lower lip, embarrassment evident in her expression. "The man will find it more difficult to do harm if there is more than one person present. Two against one. I like those odds much better than you out there all by yourself."

"Elizabeth…"

She ignored the exasperation in his tone. "With two of us working together we can finish the chores in half the time and be back here safe and sound before the sun rises."

He pushed his hat back on his head and stared down at her. "You will not let this go, will you?"

"No."

"And you will follow me if I don't take you with me?"

"Absolutely."

Thomas shook his head. "I had forgotten how stubborn you can be. Hurry. Tell Mary and get back here. I will not wait much longer."

Her feet flew across the yard.

Thomas's heart pounded in his chest, a little from a healthy dose of anxiety about running into the man who wanted only to harm Elizabeth and the people she loved, but he had to be honest and admit to himself that part of that pounding was excitement about spending the morning working with her at his side. Seven years disappeared in an instant and he remembered what his life had been like with her in it. Now he had another opportunity. He would be spending the morning with his best friend. Working. Laughing. Talking together almost like the years had never come between them. But years had passed and he had to remember that you can't go back in time—no matter how much you wish you could.

The sound of her boots clomping across the wooden porch drew his attention. He saw the door to the house fly open.

"Mamm..."

He could hear the excitement in her voice. He wasn't the only one anticipating this outing together. He knew it would only be for a few hours. He knew it wouldn't change the past and he was equally certain it couldn't change the future. Too much had happened. Too much time had passed. They were different people now with different lives.

But they had today. They had now. And that would have to be enough.

He could hear the women's voices, but it was too far to make out their words. Within seconds, Elizabeth was back on the porch and bounding down the steps toward the buggy.

Thomas leaned back in his seat and grinned.

Where was Thomas? He'd been gone for over an hour. So much for keeping a close eye on her.

She brushed the beaded sweat from her brow with the back of her hand. She hadn't had to do this much physical labor in years. It was exhilarating but also exhausting. She knew her muscles would be sore and achy tomorrow. Maybe she should have swallowed her pride and stayed home to fix breakfast after all.

Drops of icy cold water splashed her face.

Elizabeth reached up to touch the wetness while simultaneously trying to find the source.

Another splash of ice-cold wetness hit her cheek and traced a path down her neck.

She spun around and spied Thomas only a moment before he spritzed her again.

"Don't!" Elizabeth squealed and tried unsuccessfully to move out of the way.

Thomas laughed and spritzed her from the pail in his hand once again.

"Stop!" She held her hands up in front of her face. She didn't dare laugh. That is exactly what he wanted her to do and if she let him see her laugh he would come after her with no mercy. She choked on her laughter but couldn't contain a series of giggles.

"No, Thomas. Don't you dare." Trapped between the hard edge of the sink and the large, hulking man standing in front of her, she feinted one way and then the other, trying to outmaneuver him. "You're drenching my dress. I'm going to freeze to death."

Thomas barred her escape by setting down the pail, stepping closer and blocking her escape by placing an arm on either side of her against the sink. The warmth of his breath fanned her face. His smile vanished and his expression became serious.

They stared at each other, not speaking, not moving.

"Do you think I would let you freeze?" His smoldering gaze caused visible goose bumps to race up her arms.

Their emotions spoke the words their voices couldn't. The moment became heated and uncomfortable and dangerous.

Before things could move into an area neither one of them wanted, Thomas took charge. Slowly he bent to wet his hand in the pail at their feet and a mischievous grin pulled at the corners of his mouth.

"Stop it!" She laughed and pushed his hand away. "What's the matter with you? You're acting like a child."

His grin widened. "If memory serves, you used to enjoy our childish romps."

She thought her bones would melt into puddles if she stared into those blue eyes even one second more. "We are not children anymore, Thomas."

She started to turn and he clasped her upper arm so she couldn't move. "Hold still."

With his other hand he picked a piece of hay from her *kapp*. He dabbed away a drop of mud from her cheek with his thumb. "You look like you've been rolling around in the hay."

"I have been." She laughed and stepped around him. "I've cleaned four stalls and laid fresh hay in each. I should look a bit unkempt." She crossed her arms. "By the way, where have you been? You disappeared about two stalls ago."

He sobered and nodded toward the house. "I checked on the house. Made sure nothing more was broken or stolen. Picked up what I could so Mary wouldn't return to her home in disarray. I didn't see any footprints around the house. I think he came once, searched the place, and he hasn't been back."

Elizabeth looked out the barn door, her gaze

instantly landing on a familiar object. "You've put the box on the porch."

"*Ja*, just as I said I would. *Gott* willing, he will return, take the box and leave." Thomas moved past her and washed his hands in the sink. "We need to get going. Our work here is done. We told Mary we'd be home by sunrise."

Elizabeth allowed him to help her into the buggy. When he'd walked around and climbed into the seat beside her, she put a hand on his forearm. She felt his muscles flex beneath her touch and a little chill danced up her spine. "*Denki*, Thomas, for letting me come with you today."

"As if I had a choice," he teased, then snapped the reins and turned the buggy toward home. "Besides, I have to admit you were a big help. We finished our chores in record time. But you must never tell anyone," he warned. "It will not rest well with the elders if they knew I allowed you to do heavy work. They will not understand your stubbornness. Me? I know to get out of your way when you want something."

She smiled, knowing he was trying to take her mind off of the box sitting on the porch. She shot one final glance that way as their buggy moved past the house and down the dirt lane.

"Besides," Thomas said, "it is easier to keep you safe if I keep you in sight and not leave you to your own schemes."

Elizabeth heard his words but her mind remained lost in thought.

Would the man come back for the box? And if he did, would he go away, as Thomas hoped?

A restlessness tormented her. She didn't believe it would be that easy. Leave the box and have the bad guy disappear from their lives? Her feminine intuition told her a different story—and it rarely steered her wrong.

"What?" Thomas shot her a questioning look. "I know when your mind is running a mile a minute. What is bothering you? You can talk to me, Elizabeth. I will help any way that I can."

"I know, Thomas. You are a good man...and a good friend."

"So talk to me. What troubles you?"

"I need to go into town later today. I need to talk to the sheriff."

Thomas's expression sobered. "Why? The bishop asked us to let him decide when and if we bring in the *Englisch* law."

"I know. I understand. But I can't let this man get away with what he did to Hannah." She caught and held his gaze. "I can identify him, Thomas. He knows that. I don't believe he ever intended on letting me go free. He plans to kill me once he has the information he thinks I possess."

Thomas's grim expression bordered on anger. "I will not let that happen."

"I know you will try. I know you will do your

best to protect me." She patted his arm. "But you are one man—one unarmed, peaceful man who does not think in evil ways. This man will try to kill me and we both have to prepare that he might succeed."

She sat back and folded both her hands in her lap. "That is why I need to tell the police what I saw, what he looks like, while I still can. I need to help the police catch this man."

"It is not your place, Elizabeth."

"Hooey on that. Whose place is it? I saw him with his hands on Hannah's throat. I felt his hands on mine. I cannot let him get away with what he has done."

"Vengeance belongs to the Lord. Not you."

"It's not vengeance, Thomas. It's justice. Hannah was my best friend. He stole her life. He is going on with his life and not paying any consequence for his actions. How do I know he isn't going to do something like this again? And if he harms another woman and I say nothing to try and stop him, whose fault is it then?"

"What can you do? So you tell the police what he looks like. Doesn't he look like every other *Englisch* man?"

"Not any more than every Amish man looks alike."

Thomas frowned and snapped the reins, encouraging the horse to go faster.

"The police have special artists that work with

victims of crime," she explained. "In the seven years I lived in the *Englisch* world, I often saw them flash these pictures on the television. I was always surprised how much the pictures looked like the people when they found them. I must do this, Thomas. For Hannah. For myself. And for my conscience. I do not believe the Lord let me see Hannah's murder, let me live through the attempt on my own life, only to remain quiet. I believe I am meant to help solve this case."

She saw a mix of emotions play across Thomas's face. She pressed home her final point. "How is trying to protect other people from being hurt any different than you trying to protect me?"

She heard him release a heavy sigh and knew deep down he agreed with her, but she also knew he wasn't ready to defy the bishop.

"Let me think on this, Elizabeth. Pray about it. If I feel it is the right thing to do, I will speak with the bishop again."

"*Denki*, Thomas." She remained silent the rest of the ride home. It was enough for now.

SIX

It had been a pleasant, quiet, normal day, for which Elizabeth was grateful.

The *kinner* came home around noon. Isaac and Rebecca joined them for the midday meal that she and her mother had prepared. The men left for a while on horseback. Elizabeth, Mary and Rebecca had cleaned the kitchen then took the *kinner* outside to watch them play.

Rebecca darned her husband's socks. Mary kept a watchful eye on the *kinner*. Elizabeth crocheted a chain of loops to begin an afghan for Mary. She was into her second row when a huge smile tugged at her. She wished Thomas could see her now. She was doing "women's work" and doing it well.

Later, Rebecca took Rachel inside for a short afternoon nap. Benjamin busied himself filling a puddle with water and then running and splashing in the mud.

"I told you about that one," Mary said with a

laugh as she kept an eagle's eye on the youngster. "Made up of mud, mayhem and mischief."

"I think he's adorable." Elizabeth paused from her crochet work and watched the child playing.

"That he is. But you can never take your eyes off of him. He gets into the mischief of ten *kinner*, that one." Mary stood and shielded her eyes against the setting afternoon sun. "Benjamin. *Kumm.* Your *daed* will be home any minute. You have to get washed up for dinner."

Surprisingly, the boy didn't complain or hesitate. He ran up to Mary as soon as she called him. Clasping the boy with one hand, Mary looked at her daughter. "Will you be coming inside?"

"Soon. I just want to sit here and rock for a few more minutes. It's so calm and peaceful here."

Mary smiled. "*Ja*, it is. But we are also losing the day's light. Do you want me to bring you a lantern?"

"No, *denki*. I'll be okay. I'll be in in a few minutes."

"Can I stay out here with Miss Elizabeth?" Benjamin asked.

"You have to get cleaned up for dinner, young man. Now scoot." Mary playfully swatted his butt and followed the child into the house.

The shadows elongated across the yard as the sun slipped quietly behind the distant trees.

She was home. With her family. With Thomas's family. And she was happy. Truly happy.

Thank You, Lord.

Admittedly, it was a short prayer, but *Gott* knew her heart and the depth of her gratitude.

Darkness crept in like a black cat and Elizabeth knew she should move inside now and help the other two women prepare the evening meal. She started to get up when the sudden movement of the rocking chair caused her to drop a skein of yarn. She bent over to pick it up.

Whoosh!

Something flew past her ear so closely that loose tendrils of hair blew in the breeze of its wake.

Thump!

What was that? What had just happened?

Rebecca sprang to her feet and spun toward the noise. Simultaneously, Mary swung open the front door. "I heard a loud thump. Did you fall? Is everything *allrecht*?" Then her mother gasped as both women peered at the door still standing open and illuminated by the battery-powered lamps inside.

"Oh! Lord, help us." Mary pulled Elizabeth into the house, careful not to touch the door continuing to stand ajar and then yelled for Rebecca.

All three women stood stone-faced as they stared at the knife and the white paper it had embedded in the wood.

Elizabeth's blood drained out of her face and her legs wobbled beneath her.

If I hadn't dropped the yarn... If I hadn't stooped over at that very moment...that knife would have found its mark in me.

"Elizabeth." Rebecca threw a shawl around her shoulders. "You're shaking like a leaf in a storm."

"I'm fine, Rebecca." But she didn't feel fine. She stood there calmly staring at the knife in the wood of the door, not because it fascinated her but simply because she knew if she tried to move she would fall flat on her face.

"What happened? What's going on?" Thomas sprinted up the porch steps, Isaac on his heels. Within seconds, he assessed the scene and hurried the women farther inside. He pulled out the knife and the note and moved into the house, closing the door behind him.

"Was anybody hurt?" His gaze swept the room. He saw his *kinner* playing on the floor. The two older women looked shaken up, but didn't appear to be injured. When he turned his attention to Elizabeth, his heart turned over. Her deathly pale skin and glassy eyes told him all he needed to know.

He reached out and pulled her into his arms and held her tightly against him. He didn't worry about what Isaac or Rebecca thought. He didn't feel guilt at this public display of affection. He only knew that Elizabeth needed him and he was going to be there for her.

"You're all right." He cradled the back of her head against his shoulder and held her quietly until her bones stopped shaking. "Shhh. It's going to be all right. *Gott* is *gut*. No one was hurt."

After a few moments, her rigid body relaxed in his arms and her breathing slowed. When he felt she'd be able to stand on her own two feet, he released her and took a step away. He lifted her chin so he could see into her eyes.

The glazed look was gone. He saw fear. *Ja*. But he also saw anger and determination. Good for her. He could deal with her anger and determination much more than he could face her fear.

"What happened?" he asked.

All three women spoke at once.

"Wait?" Isaac raised his hand in the air. "Let Elizabeth speak."

All eyes turned toward her.

"I was rocking on the porch. It was getting dark and I decided to come inside and help with dinner, but—but…"

She paled even more, if possible. Thomas's blood boiled. He wanted to find this man and make him pay for the fear he caused. He knew he shouldn't have those feelings. He knew he'd have to repent. But maybe just this once he could repent after he taught this man to see the evil of his ways.

"A skein of yarn slid off of my lap. I leaned forward to pick it up. Something made a whooshing sound by my ear and then I heard a loud thud be-hind me. I turned to look at the door and couldn't believe what I saw." She gave a lame smile. "Who would have thought I would be grateful for hav-ing a clumsy moment? It probably saved my life. I am certain that knife was aimed at me."

She placed her hand on Thomas's wrist and nodded at the paper.

"What does it say?"

Thomas hesitated. He didn't want to upset her further.

"Tell her, Thomas." Mary put her hands on her daughter's shoulders. "She needs to know. We all do."

Several sets of eyes stared at him as he read the paper. Even the children seemed to sense the se-riousness of the moment and sat quietly watching the adults. The words hit him in the solar plexus and he found it difficult to breathe. He glanced at the worried look of the adults staring back at him. Slowly, he read the words out loud.

"'The box was filled with junk. You played me for a fool. Now you die.'"

Several hours had passed since the ominous note incident. Dinner had been eaten mostly in silence. The women cleaned up. The men finished the chores in the barn. The children were bathed and tucked into bed for the night. Isaac and Rebecca left for their own home. Everyone went about their business as usual.

But nothing was usual or normal anymore.

Elizabeth stood in the doorway of the house and listened to the quiet of the night. Even the rustling of the creatures and critters had silenced hours earlier.

Elizabeth snatched a shawl from the wooden peg on the wall and stepped onto the porch. She walked over to where her mother sat, rocking quietly.

"I thought you might need this." She tucked the shawl around her mother's shoulders.

"Denki." Mary pulled the shawl tighter.

"It's gotten quite chilly. Don't you think you should come inside?"

"In a minute."

Elizabeth sat down in the rocker next to her. The flickering light of the lantern on the small table between the chairs was their only light. "Are you okay, *Mamm*? You haven't said two words since dinner."

"I should be asking you that question." Her voice trembled and Elizabeth realized the woman had been crying.

"Oh, no. Don't be upset. I'm *allrecht*. And I'm going to continue to be *allrecht*. Don't worry." She reached over and covered her mother's hand with her own. "Look at me."

When the older woman did, Elizabeth smiled. "Really, *Mamm*. I'm fine."

Mary huffed. "Well, I'm not."

Elizabeth released her mother's hand and sat back. Both women rocked for a few minutes in silence while Elizabeth tried to choose her words with care.

"Maybe I shouldn't have come back. Maybe it would be better for everyone if I left." She held her breath, waiting for her mother's reply.

"That is nonsense. This is your home. This is where you belong." The older woman closed her eyes and leaned her head against the back of the rocker. "I probably should have tried harder to keep both of you here. Neither one of you should have ever left."

"*Mamm*, you know why I left. After my operation, I felt I had no choice."

"Yes, I do know. And I was wrong to allow it. Thomas is a *gut* man. He would have understood."

Elizabeth's eyes teared up. "That is exactly why I left. He is a good man. He would have stood by me. And then what? Would my circumstance have been fair to him?"

Mary shook her head. "I don't know. Maybe we should have left it in *Gott*'s hands instead of trying to make the decision on our own." She looked directly into Elizabeth's eyes. "If it had been only you, I would never have let you go. But I sent Hannah away, too. I believed if you were together it would be for the best. Both of you would help each other. You'd be happy…and safe."

"We were, *Mamm*. We made a *gut* life for ourselves. We made a happy life."

"Happy life? Without your family? Just the two of you alone in an evil world? Hannah is dead. And now someone is hunting you." She cradled her face in her hands. "I made a terrible mistake."

"Stop it." Elizabeth kneeled beside her mother's rocker and put her arms around the woman. "None of this is your fault. Why do you blame yourself?"

It took a few minutes for Mary to compose herself. When she looked up, grief and regret were etched in every line of her face.

"The floor is cold, child. Get up. Sit."

Elizabeth did as directed then waited for her mother to tell her why she was so upset. Instead she asked more questions.

"Do you know who this man is, Elizabeth?"

"No. Of course not. I told you I have no idea who he is."

Mary frowned. "Are you sure? You never saw him before? You never saw him with Hannah?"

"No. Never. Why?"

Mary twisted her hands in her lap. "Did Hannah ever mention this man to you? Tell you anything about him?"

"No. The first time I ever saw him or knew of

his existence was the day I saw him standing over Hannah's dead body."

"How old is he?" Mary asked.

"*Mamm*, you're scaring me. Where is this going? What do you know or think you know that I do not?"

"How old?" her mother insisted.

Elizabeth stared at her mother, her confusion growing by the second. "I'm not sure. In his early forties maybe."

Mary nodded as if she had expected that answer. "I wonder why Hannah never told you about him." The question was merely a whisper and Elizabeth felt it wasn't directed at her to answer, but was merely her mother thinking out loud.

She could not remember a time she had seen her mother so upset. She kept her tone kind and her voice soft so as not to upset her further. "If you know something, *Mamm*, please tell me."

The older woman slowly nodded her head. "I will tell you everything I know. But I have one last question."

"Anything. I have no secrets from you."

"Did Hannah act differently before her death? Did you think she might be keeping secrets from you? Did she go out without telling you where she was going or who she was seeing?"

Elizabeth seriously pondered the question. It hadn't seemed strange at the time but hindsight had twenty-twenty vision and now that she was forced to think about it, she knew her mother was right. Hannah had become quieter, kept to herself more. Elizabeth hadn't thought much about it. She knew Hannah had a new boyfriend and thought maybe her mind was on him. And, of course, they were in the middle of a move to the condo, so things were hectic. There hadn't been much time to sit and chat.

"Now that I think about it Hannah hadn't been herself lately. Quieter. A bit preoccupied maybe. But nothing that made me feel something was wrong." She stopped rocking and stared at her mother. "What do you know, *Mamm*? Do you think you know who this man is?"

Fresh tears rolled down Mary's face.

"You do!" Elizabeth's breath caught in her throat. "How do you know? Who is it, *Mamm*?"

"I believe the man is her father."

SEVEN

Elizabeth's chest felt like a fifty-pound weight was crushing the breath right out of her. She couldn't believe her ears. Hannah's father? That was absurd. Elizabeth knew Hannah's father. Her family had farmed the property right next to theirs. That's how Hannah and she had become good friends. They'd grown up together. She'd known Hannah's family as well as she'd known her own.

Was her mother losing her mind?

Poor *Mamm*. The stress must be getting to her. Was her health failing? Had more than a few gray hairs crept up on her mother in the years apart? Her heart filled with compassion. What should she do? How could she help? Did Thomas know? Was that why he had gone out of his way to take care of her mother after her father died?

She reached out and clasped her mother's hand. "Why don't you come inside now? It is dark and getting quite cold. I'll make us a cup of hot tea before we go to bed."

Mary pulled her hand away. "Don't treat me like I'm daft. I know what I know."

"I believe you." Elizabeth stood. "And I have a million questions, but I am too cold to continue talking out here. Let's go inside. I'll fix us tea and you can tell me how you know this is Hannah's father."

Her words seemed to appease her mother and the woman stood, picked up the lantern and preceded Elizabeth inside.

Elizabeth took advantage of the time it took to boil the water for tea. She busied herself setting out two mugs and putting a few cookies on a plate. On the surface she tried to keep a calm outward appearance, but her insides were a different matter. Her stomach muscles clenched so tightly they hurt. Her temples throbbed. Her mind flitted from one crazy thought to another as she tried to piece together what her mother had told her.

Once they were situated at the table, tea and cookies in front of each of them, Elizabeth smiled and broached the subject again.

"*Mamm*, I am a little confused. I know that Hannah and her father did not get along well, particularly after Hannah's mother died. That was the main reason Hannah wanted to leave home. Daniel Hofsteadter had remarried. He had young *kinner* now and he mistreated Hannah terribly. I can still remember seeing the bruises his finger-prints made on her arms. I know that the black eye he gave her was the final straw for you. That was the reason you helped us leave and secretly gave us money to hold us over while we found jobs and a place to live in Philadelphia. We both always appreciated your help."

"I didn't act alone. Your father knew about the money. He couldn't let the bishop or commu-nity know and we never spoke of it, but he knew. And approved. He loved you, Elizabeth." Mary remained quiet and sipped her tea.

"I don't understand. The Hofsteadters moved to Ohio years ago. Why would you think Han-nah's father would come back and want to harm her now? Besides, *Mamm*, I got a good look at the man who attacked me in the barn. It wasn't Hannah's father."

"Daniel Hofsteadter is not Hannah's father. Not her biological father, anyway. That is why he mis-treated her after Naomi died. He let the commu-nity believe she was his daughter. But she wasn't and he resented her for her entire life because of it." Mary shook her head. "It was such a sad situ-ation. Hannah was a wonderful little girl. I never could understand how Daniel could not see past the circumstances of her birth and love the beau-tiful child she was."

Elizabeth fell back in her chair. Her teeth chat-tered and chills raced up and down her spine, but it had nothing to do with the weather and everything to do with the intense shock attacking her system.

How could this be? Hannah had a different father? Had she known? Why had Hannah kept it a secret from her? They were best friends.

Elizabeth didn't know whether to feel sad for her friend or angry at her betrayal of their friendship.

Almost as if Mary could read her mind, she said, "Don't be upset with Hannah for not telling you. She didn't know until I told her and that wasn't until after Daniel gave her that black eye. I'm sure she would have told you someday. But some secrets get easier to cling to as time passes and it becomes harder to reveal them."

Elizabeth could tell from the look in her mother's eye that they were no longer speaking about Hannah and her father. They were talking about her and Thomas.

"Does Thomas know about Hannah's father?"

"Some of it. Just like he knows some of the reason you left. He knows Hannah had a different biological father. And he knows you left with Hannah because she was your best friend and you wanted to help her adjust to the *Englisch* world. But he doesn't know the entire truth of either situation. I had your father tell him only what I felt he needed to know to help him understand why you girls left so he could move on with his life."

She took another sip of her tea. "If I had it to do over, I would not have hidden either truth. No good can *kumm* from secrets. No good at all."

"Who is Hannah's father? How do you know him? And why do you think he would kill his own daughter? None of this makes any sense."

"All of it makes perfect sense, child." She sighed deeply and stood up. "I am going to bed now."

"But you can't! You can't drop a bombshell like that on me and then say good-night. You have to tell me what you know. We have to stop this man."

"I agree. But there is much to tell and it is late. I will tell both you and Thomas everything I know over breakfast tomorrow morning."

"Thomas?"

"Yes, Elizabeth. The time for secrets is over. We will tell Thomas the truth, all of the truth, about both you and Hannah. And with *Gott*'s help, he will know what we should do."

Elizabeth watched her mother cross the room and disappear behind her bedroom door.

Tell Thomas the truth? All of it? Maybe her mother was ready, but was she?

"You are quiet this morning, Elizabeth. Is everything all right?" Thomas stared at her over the rim of his coffee cup.

"I'm fine, Thomas. Just a little tired this morning. I didn't sleep well last night."

Assuming her lack of sleep was due to the knife in the door, he decided not to probe further. Maybe this day could begin on a more positive note.

"I changed the bandage on your horse's leg, Mary." Thomas smiled. "I do not think he will be lame. He looks like he is healing nicely."

"*Denki*, Thomas. That is good to hear." She refilled his cup and joined them at the table.

"And I have more *gut* news." He grinned like a Cheshire cat. "I spoke with our milkman and negotiated a ten-percent increase in what he is paying for our milk. It isn't much but it is a little extra."

"That is also *gut* news. Pennies add up to dollars if you are frugal with them," Mary said.

Thomas took a sip of the coffee and eyed both women. Mary seemed unusually nervous. Coupled with Elizabeth's uncharacteristic silence, Thomas knew that something was wrong and he feared it was more than the knife incident from the night before.

He noted the taut lines around Elizabeth's mouth, her downward gaze and her mother's non-stop nervous fingers tapping everything in sight.

What could be worse than having a knife thrown at you?

He glanced from one woman to the other,

pushed his empty breakfast plate away and sat back in his chair.

"Which one of you is going to tell me what is wrong?"

The women lowered their eyes and remained silent.

"Enough. I can't sit here all day. There is work to be done. What is going on between the two of you?"

Elizabeth cleared her throat. "*Mamm… Mamm* believes she knows who killed Hannah."

His eyes shot to the older woman then back to Elizabeth.

"She thinks it's Hannah's biological father." Elizabeth's hands trembled when she lifted her coffee mug.

His pulse quickened. "You know Hannah's secret?" His eyes bored into her.

She nodded. "Yes. *Mamm* told me last night. She said we are not to have any more secrets."

"Wise counsel. Secrets do no one good. The truth will always surface."

Again both women shot telling glances at each other.

"Mary, why do you think this man may be Hannah's biological father? Why would he come looking for her after all these years and then try to harm her? It makes no sense."

"Because I don't believe he came looking for

her. I believe Hannah found him. And I don't think he wanted to be found."

"Who is this man? What is his name? Is it someone from our community?" Thomas, upset by the information, threw out one question after another, giving her no time to respond.

"Thomas." Elizabeth placed a hand on top of his. "Give her a moment. She will tell us everything in her own time. This is difficult for her."

Thomas reined in his temper and they both waited for Mary to speak. When she did, he could hardly believe what she told him.

"I don't know the man's name. But I believe Naomi may have written it in one of her journals. I never read them because they were Naomi's very private, heartfelt thoughts. I found them when I was helping clean out her personal belongings after her death. Daniel didn't want them and allowed me to take them. I gave them to Hannah the day she left."

Thomas tried hard to process this new information. "Even so, Mary, it is quite a leap to believe this man would kill his own daughter just because she found him. Wouldn't he just tell her to go away and leave him alone if he didn't want to know her?"

"He wasn't a *gut* man." Mary wrung her hands and found it difficult to look at either of them. Her voice dropped to a mere whisper. "He was a rapist."

Elizabeth dropped her coffee cup. Hot coffee fell into her lap and she pushed her chair back from the table. Her mother grabbed a towel and began sopping up the hot liquid.

Elizabeth stilled her mother's hands, took the towel and finished wiping up the hot brew. Then she stared at her mother, shock and concern written all over her face. "Rapist? Hannah was a product of rape?"

Mary nodded. "It happened during our *rum-springa*. Naomi and I were best friends just as you and Hannah grew to be. We were in town together. Thinking we were all grown up and capable of making all the right decisions just because we could stay out past our curfew and were allowed to hang out in town with the other teenagers without punishment or repercussions."

Her eyes took on a sadness and far-away quality as she remembered those long-ago days.

"We were standing on the corner in front of the general store. Not doing anything special, really. Just talking." She fidgeted with her hands. "Some *Englisch* boys approached us. They were a few years older than us. One of them took a liking to Naomi. He flirted with her. He asked her to go for a walk with him in the moonlight."

Mary shook her head. "I tried to talk her out of it. I could smell liquor on his breath. And his friends seemed rowdy and liquored up, too. But she enjoyed the attention. I can still remember her saying, 'What harm is it to take a walk in the moonlight, Mary? Go home. I will see you tomorrow.' So I did."

"The next day she did not *kumm* to the house as she had said she would, so I went to see her. Her parents told me she wasn't feeling well and was in her room. When I went in to see her, she broke down sobbing and told me what had happened. He had pulled her into a field, raped her and left her lying there."

Mary cried softly. "She swore me to secrecy. She said she couldn't live with the shame if everyone knew. Shortly afterward she found out she was with child."

"Did Daniel know?" Thomas asked. He had never liked Daniel, but maybe he had been a better man than Thomas had given him credit for.

"Ja." Mary folded her hands on the table. "Daniel had proposed to Naomi once before and she had turned him down. He asked again. This time she broke down and told him what had happened. He told her he would keep her secret. That they would marry and he would raise her child as his own. Being afraid and not knowing what else to do, she accepted and they married soon after."

Mary looked at both of them with such sadness in her eyes that Thomas wondered how she could carry such a burden. "She was a good *frau* to Daniel. She was grateful for his help and determined to be the best wife she knew how to be.

But he never let her forget that she had turned down his earlier proposal and only accepted his second one because of the pregnancy, and even though he had always wanted her for his wife, he had never been able to forgive her for not loving him in return."

A heavy silence filled the room.

After several intense moments, Elizabeth spoke. "Did Naomi know her attacker's name?"

"Yes. He told her his name. He told her he lived in Pennsylvania. But she knew little more than that. I wasn't even sure she'd put the information into her journals." Mary looked at them both. "Now I wish I had read them. What if the man's name was hidden in those books and Hannah used it to track down her biological father? He may have killed Hannah so she wouldn't expose him."

Mary sobbed. "It's all my fault. I never should have told Hannah the truth. I never should have given her those journals. I couldn't stand how Hannah blamed herself for Daniel's cruelty. I couldn't continue to let her think there was something inferior or wrong with her. I thought it was important for her to understand why Daniel treated her differently from his other *kinner*."

"Did Hannah know she was a product of rape?" Thomas asked.

Mary nodded. "I told her that during *rumspringa* her mother met an older *Englisch* boy who flattered her and that things had gotten out of control. Hannah left here believing her father was a young man who had had too much to drink and didn't listen to the word *no*. Not that that was acceptable. It wasn't under any circumstances. But I believed it was a one-time incident. A terrible choice made by an intoxicated boy. Now, I'm wondering if his identity was in the pages of those journals. Maybe he wasn't just a misguided boy, but was truly an evil man. Now she's dead. And now my daughter's life is in danger, too. What have I done?"

"You have helped us more than you know, *Mamm*." Elizabeth stood and wrapped her arm around her mother's shoulders. "The police need to know about those journals. They will be able to find Hannah's real father now and figure out if he is the killer."

Thomas sprang to his feet and headed to the door.

"Where are you going?" Elizabeth asked.

Thomas grabbed his hat from the peg by the door and placed it on his head. "To talk to the bishop."

"He's been gone a long time." Elizabeth continued to break the defrosted green beans into the bowl on her lap, but she could hardly pry her eyes from watching the lane for Thomas's buggy.

"He will be gone as long as it takes." Mary continued to rock Rachel to sleep.

"What do you think will happen? Do you think the bishop will give us permission to go to the police?" Elizabeth tensed and shot a determined look at her mother. "I am going to go to the police whether the bishop gives his blessing or not. It is the right thing to do."

Mary frowned. "And you don't think the bishop knows how to do the right thing?"

"Of course I do. But just in case he doesn't…"

"Elizabeth, must you always solve all the problems of the world on your own? It is a lighter burden when you turn your troubles over to *Gott* and ask Him to guide you. Trust in Him."

She held her tongue and pondered her mother's words. When had she moved so far away from the Lord? When had she decided, consciously or not, that she needed to control her own life because she didn't like the way He did?

Had it been when she felt forced to leave Thomas, her parents and her Amish roots behind because of the medical problems He allowed her to have? Was it the empty holidays she'd spent alone, or family gatherings she had missed? Had it been not finding out about her father's death in time to attend his funeral? Or seeing Hannah's death? Or running for her own life?

Had she lost her faith completely?

She believed in *Gott*. Of course she did. But when was the last time she trusted in Him and prayed for His help and guidance?

Mary rose from the rocker, the toddler nestled in her arms. "I'm going to go in and lay her down for her nap," she whispered.

Elizabeth nodded and continued breaking the beans into the pot in preparation for making her green-bean casserole. It had always been her father's favorite...and Thomas's.

She stared up at the sky. In a few hours the sun would begin to set and breathtaking streaks of orange and gold would paint the horizon. *Gott* created such beauty in nature.

Dear Lord, I believe. Help me with my unbelief.

It was so peaceful and calm here. Unlike the bustling energy of Philadelphia. She had enjoyed the sense of excitement, the sound of the elevator trains, the bustle of the people, crowds of shoppers in the stores. She had savored every second of the experience.

But here she felt an inner peace. A quietness. A calmness. A connection with something more.

She smiled, closed her eyes and quietly rocked to and fro.

She could hear the sound of birds flying over the ice-covered pond. She could hear the rustling of the last dead leaves of autumn being tossed across the empty fields. It was so peaceful. So quiet.

Quiet!

She sat up straight and her eyes shot open.

Where was Benjamin?

She placed the pot of beans on the side table, jumped to her feet and her eyes searched the yard.

He'd been playing with his toy tractor just a minute ago not ten feet away.

Had it been just a minute ago? How long had she been lost in her own thoughts and not paying attention to the child left to her care?

"Benjamin!" She cupped her hand over her eyes and peered into the glare of the sun. No answer. No sign of the boy. Panic seized her throat and she could barely breathe.

She raced down the porch steps, stood in the middle of the yard and yelled his name again. Still no answer or sign of the child.

Had he run off into the field or snuck off near the pond? She had caught him earlier trying to walk on the ice-crusted surface, not realizing the pond wasn't frozen solid. It could have been a tragedy if she hadn't followed to see what he was up to. She'd warned him to play nearby. So where was he?

She ran as fast as she could to the pond, relieved he wasn't there and the ice was still intact, but frustrated that he still hadn't answered her calls or shown himself. She gazed out over the empty field, saw no sign of the missing child and turned back toward the house.

Where had he gone? Had somebody taken him? The fleeting thought that somehow that man had snatched him right from under her nose turned her blood to ice.

Calm down, Elizabeth. You're letting your imagination get the better of you. No one snatched the child. He's simply off playing somewhere. But where?

The barn.

Of course. He had to be in the barn.

Her feet slammed against the hard, dirt-packed ground as she raced toward the building. She burst through the door and pulled up short, shock and fear freezing her in place.

"Benjamin King! What are you doing? Why didn't you answer me?" She ran across the floor and pulled him off the third rung of the ladder to the loft. "Get down from there. You can fall and get hurt."

The fright in her voice must have sounded like anger to the child because he looked tense and teary.

"Didn't you hear me call you?"

He shook his head.

"What are you doing climbing your *daed*'s ladder? You could get hurt."

"I'm trying to get my cat. The big cat grabbed it by the neck and carried it up there." He lifted his head and pointed to the loft.

Elizabeth glanced up. She saw a mother cat with two kittens poking their heads out from beneath her peering down at them.

"That's their *mamm*, Benjamin. It's probably time for her to feed them."

"They've been up there a long time. I've been sitting here watching them and waiting for her to bring my kitty back down but she hasn't."

"She'll bring your kitten down when she's ready. That doesn't mean you should climb up after it."

Benjamin sniffed and tears rolled down his cheeks. "My kitty is going to fall if I don't get her down. She's going to get hurt."

"Her *mamm* won't let that happen."

"She will. She can't always be looking. You weren't always looking or you would have seen me come into the barn and you wouldn't be so mad at me."

The corners of her mouth turned down.

Out of the mouths of babes.

"Okay. I'll go up and get the kitten. But only if you promise me you will never, ever try to climb into the loft again. I don't care if the mother cat takes her babies up there. You, young man, are not allowed to follow them. Understand?"

Benjamin nodded vigorously and dragged his hand across his tear-streaked face and dripping nose.

Elizabeth started to climb the ladder.

What are you doing? Are you crazy? You think that mamma cat is going to just let you snatch her kitten?

She stopped and decided to go back down when she looked below and saw Benjamin's grinning face staring up at her.

"You can do it, Miss Elizabeth. You're almost to the top. You can get my kitty for me."

Great! How was she going to say no to such an endearing, hopeful little face? She wasn't.

She was on the next-to-the-last rung when she heard an ominous cracking sound. She looked down at her foot and her eyes widened. A wide gap in both sides of the ladder rail told her the wood had been cut. When she had moved her hands up the rail and pulled her weight up the rung, it splintered beneath her hold and the top of the ladder split and folded in on itself. The wood hit her on the head and the speed of the collapse made it impossible for her to regain safe footing.

Elizabeth tried to grab the edge of the loft but had no time to save herself. Within seconds she felt herself hurtling backward through the air and she screamed. Pain was her last conscious thought as her body slammed into the barn floor.

EIGHT

Elizabeth's body floated on a cloud. Soft. Welcoming. So why did every inch of her body ache? She tried to open her eyes but they refused to obey her brain's command.

Where am I? What happened?

She heard voices. Muffled. Far away. But definitely voices.

She tried again to open her eyes. They fluttered once, twice, then finally she was able to see.

She wasn't on a cloud. She was lying on a soft mattress. A battery-powered lamp rested on the table beside her bed. She glanced around the room. This was her room. Temporarily, of course. She was in the *dawdi haus*. But how did she get here and why did her muscles ache?

Then she remembered.

Everything.

She sprang upright and then moaned and grabbed her forehead as pain shot through her temple.

A light tap and then the door opened.

"*Gut*. You're awake." Thomas stepped into the room with her *mamm* and Benjamin in tow.

Benjamin ran to her side, his little hand patting her arm. "I'm sorry, Miss Elizabeth. I didn't want you to fall. I shouldn't have asked you to go up and get my kitty."

Elizabeth gingerly turned to look at him and tried to ignore the sharp pain that seized her every time she tried to move her head. She patted his tiny hand. "It's *allrecht*, Benjamin. You didn't do anything wrong."

"Did you get hurt?" His lower lip quivered.

"*Neh*, sweetheart. I got a couple of little bumps and bruises, but I will be fine."

Her answer made him grin.

"Okay, *sohn*. I told you I would let you see her. Now you have and you can see that she is going to be *allrecht*. Go with Miss Mary and get ready for bed. I will be up shortly."

Mary touched her daughter's hand. "Are you truly okay? The doctor said you would be *allrecht* but doctors don't know everything."

"Doctor?"

"*Ja*. Thomas paid extra for Dr. Bridges to make a house call. He left a little over an hour ago."

Elizabeth tried to sit up but her mother put a hand out to stop her. "*Neh*, you rest. I will help Thomas get the *kinner* ready for bed and then I will be back. I will bring some soup. You have been asleep for several hours. You missed dinner."

With a final pat on her arm, her mother hurried out of the room.

Thomas stepped out of the shadows. He handed Rachel over to Mary and then approached the side of the bed.

They stared at each other in silence. So many things to say. So difficult to find the words to say them.

"Are you really *allrecht*?" Thomas's expression held more than concern. If she didn't know better, she would have thought he was afraid.

"I'm fine." She sat up and leaned against the headboard. "My head aches a little if I move too fast." She moved her arms and her legs. "I'm achy here and there. Probably have a bruise or two. But I will be fine."

Thomas's face still looked pale and his features grim.

"Really, Thomas. Don't worry. I'm fine."

He nodded and pulled over a straight-back chair. "May I sit for a minute?"

"Of course." She reached up, straightened her *kapp* and smoothed the apron still in place over her dress. "*Denki* for calling the doctor out here. I am sure it was less frightening for my *mamm* than if I had to go into town or to the hospital."

"What happened, Elizabeth? Were you truly foolish enough to climb into the loft for a kitten?"

"Better me than Benjamin." She bristled beneath his criticism even though she knew it came from fear not anger. "The boy tried to climb the ladder to the loft after his kitten. I took him off the lower rungs and went up in his place." She groused under her breath. "I should have left the kitten up there."

Thomas scratched his beard. "I don't understand. The ladder was brand-new. It should not have had a broken rung."

Elizabeth sighed. "Someone sawed ninety percent through the sides of the top railing bordering the last few rungs. Any adult weight would snap it as they climbed. I didn't see the damage until it was too late and I didn't have time to try and break my fall because the top of the ladder collapsed in on itself."

"Sawn through? Are you sure?" Shock claimed his features. "You could have been killed."

"But I wasn't." She smiled even though it took great effort. "A little banged-up, maybe, but okay."

"Falling from that height and not getting hurt? *Gott* is *gut.*"

"What can I say? The little extra weight around my hips must have padded my landing."

Thomas didn't laugh. "It isn't funny. You could have broken your back or, *Gott* forbid, snapped your neck."

"But I didn't."

"It was that man again, *ja?*"

"Probably."

"Why did he saw through the ladder? What

made him think you would be climbing into the loft?"

Elizabeth sent him a steady gaze but stayed silent.

His eyes registered understanding. "The fall wasn't meant for you. It was meant for me." He squeezed her hand. "I am so sorry."

"Sorry that you didn't fall or get maimed or killed?" She smiled. "I'm not."

"Why is he doing this terrible thing? Why would he want me dead?"

Elizabeth, moved with compassion for the confusion and hurt she saw in his eyes, wanted to wrap her arms around him in comfort. But she knew that was something she shouldn't do... couldn't do. Thomas was no longer hers to comfort, depend on, or love. She'd have to be cautious and keep reminding herself of that fact. She tried to explain.

"Because he is afraid. He is angry and not thinking clearly. He is acting in desperation."

"What is he afraid of? We have not harmed him."

"But he knows we can." Elizabeth swung her legs over and sat on the edge of the bed. "He believes I know his identity and, thanks to *Mamm*, I believe he's right. We do. I believe this man is Hannah's biological father. He thinks I have the proof. Maybe the journals? He does not know who

I have told so he is trying to destroy everyone in close proximity to me."

Thomas waved his hand in the air and paced the floor. "Why doesn't he just shoot us all and be done with it?"

"*Neh*, Thomas. Don't say such a thing!"

"Well? Would it be worse than this slow torture he is putting us through?"

"He wants to make it look like accidents so the police don't get involved. He does not want an investigation. He wants to make sure his secret stays secret."

"Throwing a knife at the door with a note that says he wants you dead isn't an accident in my mind."

"I told you. He's desperate…and afraid. He isn't thinking logically and that makes him even more dangerous."

"He is a coward hiding in the shadows."

Elizabeth did not see Thomas get angry often. He was angry now and she empathized with his current frustration.

"I am so sorry, Thomas."

He had a puzzled expression on his face. "Sorry? For what? You have done nothing wrong."

"I brought danger with me when I came home. I am afraid someone is going to get hurt, somebody that I love, somebody completely innocent in all of this mess. And I will be to blame."

"Nonsense. If anyone does get hurt, it will

be that man's doing, Elizabeth, not yours." He stopped pacing and stood squarely in the middle of the room. His stature erect, his shoulders back, as if bracing for an attack, his determination was evident in every muscle. *"Ich verschreck net graad."*

"I don't scare easily, either." She parroted him in English instead of repeating his Amish words. "But I am not foolish enough to ignore the danger we're in."

"Neither am I," Thomas said. "It is up to all of us to do what we must do to make sure that nothing happens to harm anyone. And we will."

A glimmer of hope fluttered in her chest. "Did you speak with the bishop?"

"Ja. He is coming here first thing in the morning. He wants to go with us to speak with the sheriff."

"Then he agrees it is the right thing to do?"

Thomas nodded. "When I showed him the note and the knife, he knew we had no choice. We must do everything we can as a community to keep you safe and try to stop this man."

"Does he know what happened here today?"

"Neh. When we tell him in the morning, he will be more determined than ever to stop this man."

Mary appeared in the open doorway with a tray of hot soup and tea.

"Gut," she said, not at all apologetic for listening in on their conversation. "I told you the bishop

would do the right thing, Elizabeth. Now *kumm*. Have something to eat before it gets cold." She glanced at Thomas. "The *kinner* are in their beds and waiting for you to say *gut necht*."

"*Denki*, Mary. I will go to them now." He paused in the doorway and glanced back at Elizabeth. "It is *gut* that you came back to us. Do not ever question it. Get some rest. We will talk again in the morning."

She watched him leave. Her *mamm* gestured for Elizabeth to join her in the kitchen. She reached the kitchen just as she heard the sound of the front door closing.

Thomas had told her the bishop and the rest of the community wanted her to stay and would help to keep her safe. No wonder she considered this place her home and these people her family. Even Thomas wanted her to stay despite the pain she had caused him years ago. He'd made that evident by doing everything in his power to keep her safe. Would it be selfish of her to stay and possibly bring more harm to their community? Or would it be selfish to leave, depending only on her own wits and discounting the feelings of everyone who had ever cared for her?

She stared at the closed door.

Despite the problems and danger, everyone in the community seemed to want her to stay.

Even Thomas.

And her heart filled with hope.

* * *

Thomas stepped quietly into Rachel's room and crossed to her bed. He stared down at his sleeping daughter, shining the light from the portable lamp he carried across her form. She was lying on her back, her right arm carelessly slung over her head, her long lashes curled at the edges, her cheeks blushing a soft rosy hue against the tender softness of her cheeks, her lips puckered as she sucked on an imaginary pacifier in her dreams. Lost in sleep, she looked so much like her mother.

A pang of grief seized him.

Two years since he'd been able to sit with Margaret in the quiet of the evening and share the details of his day, enjoy the warmth of her home cooking, smell the lemon freshness of her hair and feel her petite form curled in his arms in bed at night.

Two years.

Sometimes it seemed as if it had been only yesterday. Sometimes it seemed like another life, a thousand years ago.

Rachel would never know her mother's love. But she would know her mother. He would speak of her often and keep her alive in the child's mind.

Thomas gently pressed his lips against his sleeping daughter's forehead and quietly left the room.

He wasn't surprised to see light shining beneath Benjamin's door. He pushed the door ajar. The battery-powered lamp on the table beside his bed lit the room. A huge tented mound of blankets lit from the inside by flashlight let him know instantly that his *sohn* was not asleep, but on some incredible imaginary adventure beneath the tent-like structure.

Where did this child get his never-ending energy? Not from him, he thought, as he placed a hand over the yawn that claimed him.

"Benjamin, *kumm*. It is time to sleep."

Thomas lifted the edge of the covers and was momentarily taken aback. Benjamin had used a feather duster braced against a block of wood from the fireplace to brace the blankets up as a tent. The child sat cross-legged and crouched over, the flashlight he held shining its beam upward on his chin and highlighting his small freckled face in the cloaked darkness of the blankets.

Thomas couldn't help but laugh. What was an Amish man to do with so much creativity? How was he to direct his son to use *Gott*'s gifts in a more practical way? He scratched his chin beneath his beard. Maybe that wasn't his job. Maybe his job was to encourage his boy to follow *Gott*'s direction in his life no matter where that path might lead. At one time, Amish people never wore bright colors. It changed over the years. Maybe his Benjamin would bring more change—good, creative change—to his people. *Gott* created this wonderful, intriguing, energetic boy. Thomas could hardly wait to see what *Gott* had planned for his *sohn*'s life.

"Look, *Daed*." Benjamin grinned at his father. "There is a great storm coming. A tornado with darkness and winds. I have built a safe place inside this tent for the animals." Benjamin held up the hand carved cow and horses that Thomas had crafted for the boy last Christmas.

He smiled and his heart seized. He loved this little boy so much. He had lost Margaret, but *Gott* had blessed him with two beautiful, unique *kinner*. His gratitude knew no bounds.

"Let's put the animals to sleep." Thomas took the wooden toys from his hands. "And it is past time for you to go to sleep, too. Have you said your prayers?"

Benjamin nodded. "Miss Mary and I prayed together."

"Gut." He removed the duster and wood from beneath the blankets and again smiled at the child's creativity.

"We prayed for *Grossmammi* Rebecca and *Grossdaedi* Isaac," Benjamin said as he crawled to the top of his bed and flopped his head down on his pillow. "And for *Grossmammi* and *Gross-*

daedi in Florida. And for you and Rachel. And I even prayed for Miss Mary and Miss Elizabeth."

"I am sure *Gott* was happy to hear from you tonight."

"I even asked *Gott* to say *gut necht* to *mamm* and tell her I love her and I miss her."

Thomas paused, a bittersweet pang stealing his breath. "You are a *gut sohn*. Now close your eyes and get some sleep." He ran his hand across Benjamin's silky hair and tucked the blanket around his shoulders.

He doused the lights and stepped out of the room.

He entered his bedroom, crossed to the small chest at the end of the bed, sat down and pulled off his boots. He ran his hand across the wood. He'd made this chest as a wedding gift for Margaret to keep her quilts in after they had married.

He slid open a drawer to remove fresh clothes for tomorrow and his hand fell upon a crisp, white prayer *kapp*. He pulled it out and sat back down on the chest.

This is Margaret's kapp. I kept it for Rachel so she would have something of her mother, so I could hold it in my hands and show it to her when I talk to her about what a wunderbaar *woman her mother was.*

He twisted the fabric in his hands. The edges of his mouth turned down.

What is wrong with me tonight? Why am I feel-

ing more nostalgic than normal? What is it that bothers me?

Gently, he folded the fabric.

Elizabeth. That is why.

He placed the *kapp* back into the corner of the top drawer.

My mind wanders to another woman and I feel guilty and afraid I will forget my Margaret.

His eyes burned.

Please, Margaret. Don't be upset with me. I cannot help it. You and I spoke many times about Elizabeth. Neither of us ever believed she'd be back home again. But she is. And my heart remembers days past no matter how much my mind cautions against it.

Thomas put on fresh long johns and climbed beneath the covers. He placed his hand on the empty pillowcase beside him.

I will not forget you, Margaret. And I will continue to speak often and lovingly of you to our kinner.

He rolled onto his back and spoke aloud in the darkness.

"I think you would have liked her, Margaret. You are very different women, but deep down your hearts are the same." He placed his arm across his forehead and whispered his deepest fears. "But I am frightened. Bad things are happening. Things I cannot control. What if I cannot keep her safe? What if she knows it and decides to run away again? My heart broke when I lost you. I am afraid of what will happen to the last shards of my heart if Elizabeth runs and I lose her again."

He stared into the darkness for long patches of time. Then he began to pray.

NINE

Thomas coughed. Restlessly he rolled over in bed. His mind tried to wake him while his tired body wanted only to burrow farther beneath the covers. It couldn't possibly be time to get up. Hadn't he just fallen asleep?

He opened his eyes and turned his head toward the window.

Pitch-black.

Exactly what he'd expect in the middle of the night. He glanced at his wind-up clock. Three thirty.

He was right. It wasn't time to get up yet.

So what was it that disturbed him?

A dream must have pulled him from his slumber. He plumped his pillow, settled into a comfortable position on his side and gave himself permission to return to sleep.

Until he coughed again.

He sat up in bed.

His chest tightened and his eyes burned. He

grabbed a flashlight he kept in the drawer beside his bed and aimed the light toward the bedroom door.

Smoke!

A light gray mist—a toxic mist—seeped under the door and floated into the air.

Thomas jumped out of the bed. Grabbing his shirt and pants from the peg beside the bedroom door, he dressed faster than he knew possible and rushed into the hall. The thicker, denser smoke in the hallway knocked his heart rate up a notch. He ran with as much speed as he could muster to Benjamin's room.

"Get up, *sohn*. We must go. Now!" He lifted the boy from the bed, clasping the confused and half-asleep child in his arms, and raced for his daughter's room.

Rachel was already awake. She was standing on the bed, rubbing her eyes and crying.

He snatched her up.

"Hold fast to my neck. We must hurry and get out of here." With a child in each arm he bolted toward the stairs. The closer he got to the stairwell, the thicker the smoke. A blast of heat met him at the top of the stairs, but thankfully, he did not see any fire. As he moved cautiously but quickly down the stairs into the heavier smoke, the three of them struggled with spasms of coughing.

Benjamin started to cry.

"Shhh, little ones. It's going to be *allrecht*.

We're going to be outside in a minute. Bury your faces in my shirt so you don't smell the smoke."

Both children did as he instructed.

A sense of relief washed over him when he made it to the front door. Before he could lower Benjamin to the floor so he could free his hand to clasp the doorknob, it flew open.

"Oh, thank You, *Gott*." Elizabeth reached over the threshold and pulled Rachel from his arms. "Hurry. We have to get the *kinner* outside."

Thomas, both arms clasping Benjamin against his chest, ran out the door behind her.

Thomas cleared the porch and was about fifty feet from the house before he dared to stop. He placed Benjamin down and stood beside Elizabeth and Rachel.

He looked back. Thick black smoke plumed to the heavens. The ominous whooshing and crackling of the bright orange flames filled the night air and the intense heat seared his face despite the distance from the blaze. The acrid smell scorched his throat and burned his eyes. One quick glance at the others and he saw the heat affected them, too, noting their red cheeks from the heat and tears streaming down their faces.

Thomas quickly examined both his children to make sure they were unharmed. Only then did he take a deep, cleansing breath to try and clear his smoke-filled lungs.

"What—what happened?" he asked, choking on his words.

He looked again at the burning *dawdi haus*.

"Mary? Where is Mary?" A sense of panic laced his words. He moved to run toward the house and Elizabeth grabbed his arm.

"She's out. She's safe."

"Are you sure you and your *mamm* are unharmed?" His eyes searched Elizabeth from head to toe for any injury and found none. "How did this happen? Did the wind knock over a lantern?"

Before Elizabeth could reply they heard a repetitive, sharp clanging sound pierce the stillness of the night air. Thomas glanced over at the far end of his porch and saw Mary ringing the triangle over and over again, calling the community for help.

Shortly after Mary had stopped ringing the triangle, the nearest neighbors began to arrive quickly followed by others.

The closest ones ran through the icy fields. Others arrived in buggies. They came over the hills in droves, sleep long gone from their minds.

Thomas knew the fire department wouldn't be far behind. Many of his Amish neighbors were volunteer firemen for the Sunny Creek unit. But someone had to take charge and organize the people who were here now. Rachel was cradled safely in Elizabeth's arms. Thomas quickly kneeled before his crying boy.

"I know this is a scary thing, Benjamin, but try not to be afraid. No one is hurt. *Gott* is protecting us." He glanced up at Elizabeth and then back to his son. "I need you to stay here with Miss Elizabeth while I go and help the other adults put out the fire." He grabbed his son's shoulders and made eye contact. "Do you understand? I mean it. You must not move from this spot unless Miss Elizabeth tells you to. This is not a time for you to wander away."

The boy nodded.

Thomas stood up. "I've got to get Mary off of that porch. She's too close to the fire."

"Look," Elizabeth pointed in that direction. "She's coming this way now."

Assured that all his loved ones were safe, he placed Benjamin's hand in Elizabeth's. "I have to go. Please take care of my *kinner.*"

"I will, Thomas. Be safe."

He turned and ran toward the crowd, which had already formed a water line from the trough by the horse corral. They were handing buckets of water as quickly as possible from one man to another in an attempt to put out the flames.

Isaac suddenly appeared out of the darkness. "*Mein Gott*, what has happened? Is everyone safe?"

His clothes unkempt and hair disheveled, he wore a sleepy look of disbelief on his face. Rebecca ran up right behind him.

"Where are the children?" she asked.

Thomas pointed toward Elizabeth and Mary. Rebecca ran in their direction.

Thomas slapped Isaac on the shoulder. "*Kumm* with me. I've got two hoses in the barn." Within minutes, both men were dousing the flames with streams of water but one look at the destruction and Thomas knew it was a losing battle. The *dawdi haus* was lost. The most important thing now was to keep the flames from reaching the main house. Already Thomas could see a couple of the panels of siding on his front porch melted and scorched.

Sirens wailed in the distance, growing louder by the second. Within minutes red and blue strobe lights flashed across the yard and flitted across the still standing porch of the main house. Help had arrived. It was one of the most welcome sights Thomas could remember seeing in a long time.

Elizabeth took her first deep relaxing breaths. The firemen extinguished the flames. Only misty white smoke hovering above smoldering ashes remained. She adjusted her back against the tree she'd been leaning on in an attempt to get more comfortable. Thankfully, the flames hadn't claimed the main house. She hoped she'd be able to move the children out of the cold and into the warmth of the house soon.

"Do you want me to take her?" Rebecca whispered, gesturing toward Rachel, who was asleep in Elizabeth's arms. "You haven't had a break for hours. You must be exhausted."

Elizabeth glanced down at Benjamin, his head lying on her thigh while he slept. She adjusted Rachel's sleeping body in her arms and smiled. She was falling in love with these children and at this moment couldn't think of anyplace else she wanted them to be.

"No thank you, Rebecca. They're fine. I don't want to wake them."

Rebecca smiled, a knowing look in her eyes. "If you change your mind, I will be sitting on what's left of the porch with Mary. She won't move. She insists on sitting in one of the rocking chairs, and even though I offered to move it off the porch and over closer to you, she still insists on staying on the porch. What does she think? If she sits there, the fire won't touch the house?"

Elizabeth chuckled. "It is one of her favorite things to do, rock on a porch and watch the world pass by. Now that the firemen have contained the blaze, it probably makes her feel safe to sit there, like some things are still normal in this crazy world."

Rebecca placed a comforting pat on her shoulder. "I am sure you are right." She leaned over and placed a mug of hot tea on the ground beside her. *"Denki."*

"I'll go and keep her company. I could use a little 'normal' right now, myself."

She watched the woman cross the yard and join her mother on the porch.

The scent of cinnamon teased her nostrils and was a welcome change to the acrid smell of burned wood. Elizabeth glanced down at the hot mug of tea. Now if she could only figure out a way to pick it up without waking Rachel.

"Let me help."

Thomas.

What a welcome sight! She'd tried to keep track of him during the fire, but in the darkness with so many men fighting the flames she hadn't been able to single him out of the crowd. Now he stood near her feet, the hint of dawn lighting the sky behind him.

Her eyes took a quick inventory for any burns or injuries.

He appeared unhurt.

Denki, Gott.

Black soot and sweat covered him from top to toe. He wore weariness and concern in every crease in his face, but stood before her confident and strong. A far cry from the tall, lanky young man she had left seven years ago. Farming, hard physical labor and a few years had honed his muscles and finished his transition from boy to man.

Dirty. Unkempt. Tired. And she'd never found him more attractive.

Thomas crouched down beside her and lifted his sleeping daughter from her arms.

"Put her here," Elizabeth whispered and scooted to make room on the quilts she had thrown on the cold ground while trying not to disturb Benjamin. She adjusted the other quilts she had placed over the three of them to keep them warm and lifted an edge for Thomas.

He settled on the ground beside her and covered his daughter's back with the excess blanket to keep her warm.

"I'm sorry, Thomas."

"Again, you apologize. For what?"

She gestured to the still smoking ashes of what had once been part of his home. "You've lost everything."

"Not everything. The people I love are unharmed. The main house is untouched. We are fortunate my parents are in Sarasota for the winter. You and Mary can move into their rooms on the main floor. I will have a new *dawdi haus* built before they return and all will be well." He smiled at her, his teeth appearing extra white against the black soot smeared on his skin. "You are the one who lost everything. I'm sorry, Elizabeth. There was no way to recover any of your belongings."

"That's all they were, Thomas. Belongings. Nothing that can't be replaced." She smiled back at him. "Here. You look like you need this more than I do." She picked up the mug and handed it to him.

He lifted the cup to his lips, took a long, healthy swallow and handed it back.

"*Denki.* I needed that. My throat is dry from breathing in all that smoke."

He leaned his head back against the tree trunk and closed his eyes.

As seconds of silence became minutes, Elizabeth thought he had fallen asleep until he spoke.

"The fire wasn't caused by an overturned lantern, was it?" He still didn't open his eyes or move.

"No."

"When is this going to stop?" The question seemed more rhetorical than one that demanded an answer. More a whisper of pain and troubled thoughts.

"When we do what we have to do to stop this man. *Ja?*"

Both Elizabeth and Thomas turned their heads to see the speaker. Bishop Schwartz, his face as sooty as Thomas's, his features as drawn and tired, stared down at them.

"Bishop Schwartz, I didn't see you in the chaos and confusion." Thomas stood, stretched out a hand and shook the elderly man's in gratitude. "*Denki* for coming."

"Where else would I be? You know we band together and help our own, Thomas."

"*Ja.* 'Tis true."

"And it is time now for the community to band together and get rid of the weed that has infiltrated our lives before any more damage occurs."

"I wanted to speak with you, Bishop." Elizabeth gently eased Benjamin's head off of her leg and stood up, too. "I was going to ask Thomas to bring me over later today."

"Speak, child."

"Yesterday afternoon, in the barn…"

"*Ja, ja*, I know. The sawn-through ladder. I was told and I am grateful you were not seriously injured."

"Then tonight…the fire…" She could sense Thomas tense beside her, almost as if he knew what she was about to say. The bishop shot her a quizzical look but did not interrupt.

"I don't want anyone hurt."

"Of course not, child. No one wants anyone hurt."

"But being here is dangerous for everyone. This man is intent on destroying me and everyone I come in contact with. I could not bear it if my being here causes someone to get injured or perhaps lose their life." She gestured toward the smoldering ashes of the *dawdi haus*. "I have already caused Thomas the loss of a large part of his home."

"What are you trying to say, Elizabeth?" the bishop asked.

"I wonder if it is time for me to leave—past time—before anything more happens."

She wrapped her arms tightly around her trembling body, unsure whether her shuddering was from the cold or from anticipation of his answer.

The bishop arched an eyebrow. "Did you set the fire?"

"Neh."

"Do you believe you are *Gott* or that you have the power to control another's actions?"

Elizabeth's cheeks flamed and she lowered her eyes. "Of course not."

"This is the second time I have heard this question from you and I do not want to hear it again." He spoke sternly but his tone held compassion as well. "What Thomas told you before is correct. You cannot solve problems by running away from them. They only follow you and cause more problems." He stepped closer and placed a comforting hand on her shoulder.

"Gott will help us deal with this man. I have prayed for His guidance. I suggest you do the same. I do not believe when He answers your prayers that He will tell you to leave your family and community now that you have found your way home. Understand?"

Elizabeth nodded.

"Gut. Now I am going home to clean up, change my clothing and take a brief rest. I am not as young as I used to be." He chuckled. "Although I

held my own with the younger men fighting that fire." He gestured over his shoulder. "I am sure I will feel it in my bones today. But that will be a *gut* thing. A little ache in my bones will remind me that I am still alive and useful."

He smiled at Elizabeth. "I will return later this morning to pick you up. It is time we speak to the sheriff together. He will do what he needs to do and I will do what I need to do. When we return, I will call the men to a community meeting. We will form a plan and develop a schedule so our community is protected and everyone is kept as safe as possible while the *Englisch* law brings this man to justice."

"*Gut* to hear, Bishop," Thomas said.

The bishop nodded toward both of them and left.

Thomas looked at her and shook his head. "Will there ever be a time, Elizabeth, when you will stop believing that running away is the answer?"

Her eyes widened and she couldn't contain the anger and frustration in her voice. "Do you think it would be easy to leave? You act like running away is a selfish thing."

"Isn't it?"

"No!" She railed at him. "Leaving is hard. Sometimes it is the hardest thing you ever do in your entire life, but you do it. Not for yourself. But for the good of others."

"And you know what is best for others?" He threw his hands up in the air in frustration. "It is not your place to play *Gott*, Elizabeth. What gives you the right to make people's decisions for them? *Neh*, it is not your right." He stared her down. "It was never your right."

His jaw tightened and his eyes flashed his pain.

Her *mamm* and Rebecca had approached when they saw the bishop walk over to speak to them. Now they stood quietly to the side, watching. The discomfort in their body language and the way they both shot glances everywhere but at her told Elizabeth that they'd overheard their argument.

Mary spoke first. "We will take the children inside now. It is cold out here and it is time they get some warm food in their bellies."

Rebecca was already lifting Rachel into her arms.

"Take your time. Finish your conversation," Mary said. "Rebecca and I will have a hot breakfast waiting for both of you when you come inside."

After they left with the children, Elizabeth glanced over at Thomas.

Now is the time to tell him. Make him understand why you hurt him so much.

She wanted to. The words rested on the tip of her tongue. But she couldn't. Not yet. Maybe not ever. After all these years, what would it change?

Thomas looked like he was also struggling to

find words that might ease the tension between them. Finally, he spoke.

"We are fortunate it is *Gott*'s will that the main house remains standing. We will all have a roof over our heads, warmth against the cold, food to eat. *Gott* is good."

His acceptance of the situation, his laid-back attitude, made her snap.

"Is that what you think, Thomas? This was *Gott*'s will? And that's enough for you? No anger. No fear. No remorse. And, of course, let's not even consider that nasty word *vengeance*. After all, the Amish are perfect people in a perfect world. They never blame anyone for anything. They just plop it in *Gott*'s hands and go on with everyday business. Right?"

She practically screamed the words at him and then covered her mouth with her hands. She couldn't believe what she'd said. It was fear talking. And anger. Frustration. Maybe a little bit of hopelessness. Definitely helplessness. But she, too, was Amish. She didn't believe those horrible words that poured out of her mouth, did she? Had she been gone from the Amish so long that her heart had hardened and her faith had disappeared?

Thomas stared at her long and hard. When he spoke, weariness and maybe even a little resignation laced his words.

"Do you think being Amish makes me, what— less than human? That I have no feelings? I have feelings, Elizabeth. Too many feelings some-times." His eyes flashed with anger.

"I didn't mean…"

"Neh?" He paced back and forth and then pulled to an abrupt stop in front of her. He slapped a hand against his chest, practically spitting his words out. "I *feel*, Elizabeth. The grief I felt—deep, soul-wrenching grief—when I lost my Margaret brought me to my knees too many nights to count." He stomped his foot and pointed his arm toward the horizon. "And that evil man who did this? I am not ashamed to say I am angry—red-hot, boiling-in-my-very-soul angry. Do you think it is easy for me to try to keep everyone I care about, everyone who claims my heart, free from the clutches of this evil man?"

He took several deep breaths and struggled to control himself. When he turned to look at her, she could see something had changed. When he spoke again, his tone of voice had softened. "And I've known sorrow, Elizabeth—dull, aching pain that I have felt for years. It started the day you left me."

"Thomas." Her heart seized as she witnessed the raw emotions flashing across his face. She wanted to reach out to comfort him but forced herself to remain still.

"How do you see me?" His eyes searched hers. "I am *human*, Elizabeth, as well as Amish. I hurt and get angry and suffer and, *ja*, sometimes I feel afraid and unsure of myself."

He clasped her hands in his.

"But I have also known great joy. The day I held Benjamin in my arms for the first time and later, Rachel, I thought *Gott* had blessed me with a little piece of heaven." He smiled into her eyes. "I had a *wunderbaar* life with a good, solid, kind, loving woman. I have experienced laughter, and happiness...and love. So far it has been a *gut* life. Ups and downs, but *gut*."

His eyes darkened with an emotion that frightened yet exhilarated her at the same time. He still had feelings for her. Deep feelings. She couldn't pretend anymore that they were merely friends.

"Sometimes it is difficult for me to say 'It is *Gott*'s will' and mean it." He chuckled mirthlessly. "Many times when I am frustrated and, *ja*, maybe even mad at Him, I have told *Gott* that we need to have a long talk when we meet in person so He can explain why He allowed my life to unfold the way it did." He softly traced the pad of his thumb down her cheek. "But then sometimes He surprises me. He answers my prayers before I even pray them."

He pulled her close.

"I have lived long enough to look back on my life and see how each thing that happened, *gut* or bad, led to another. How I wouldn't have turned down one path if *Gott* hadn't allowed an obstacle to block another."

He smiled down on her.

"So, *ja*, I trust *Gott*, Elizabeth. With everything."

He pressed his lips against her forehead for several heartbeats, then stepped back.

"*Gott* is waiting for you to trust Him, too, *lieb*. Think about it. Better still, pray about it."

He released her and walked toward the house.

TEN

The autumn sun bathed her cheeks in warmth despite the chill in the air. Elizabeth searched the sky. Gray clouds looming on the horizon warned of the first snowstorm of the season quickly approaching. She pulled her shawl tightly around her shoulders.

"I thought I might find you out here." Her mother approached, pulling her own shawl tighter as she came and stood beside her on the porch.

"I can't believe the *dawdi haus* is gone." Elizabeth glanced over at the blackened pile of ashes. "There is nothing left, *Mamm*. Thomas built the *dawdi haus* and now he's lost everything in it, furniture, house goods, everything."

"*Neh*, not everything. What matters to his heart is still here, alive and well. People matter to Thomas. *Kinner.* Family. Friends. Things can be replaced and rebuilt, *ja*?" She smiled and wrapped an arm around her daughter's waist. "How did your conversation go with Thomas after we left? Did you finally tell him the truth about why you left?"

"No." She released a deep sigh. "I wanted to. I almost did."

"What stopped you?"

"What good would it do? It happened seven years ago. How can it possibly matter now?"

"It matters to Thomas."

"Why?"

"Because it is an open wound that has not been able to heal. He has never understood. He has blamed himself for you leaving, but he's not even sure what he blames himself for." Mary tilted Elizabeth's chin with her index finger. "You must tell him, child. He has a right to know."

"It will make me look like I am making excuses or asking his forgiveness."

"Aren't you?"

"Yes." She smiled at her mother. "And no."

A perplexed expression flashed across Mary's face.

"Yes, of course, I wish his forgiveness," Elizabeth said. "I caused him so much pain and my leaving was supposed to do just the opposite. But I am not going to use my medical condition as an excuse or to play on his sympathies. If I had it to do over again, I would make the same choice."

Mary tilted her head and her mouth fell open. "You would?"

Elizabeth laughed. "After I told Thomas everything, of course. That part I would do differently. I wouldn't have made him wonder all these years. I would have made sure he understood my choice."

Mary nodded. "*Gut*. It is nice to know living in an *Englisch* world for so many years has not hardened your heart so much that you cannot see the mistakes you have made. We both have made mistakes. It is time now to tell the truth. No more secrets."

"No more secrets."

Mary hugged her daughter.

"Where is Thomas?" Elizabeth glanced over Mary's shoulder toward the house and then looked out toward the barn.

Mary smiled. "He knew he was not the only one who lost everything in the fire. So he left to try and fix it."

"What do you mean?"

"Everything you owned in this world was in your suitcases inside the *dawdi haus*. You have nothing left but the clothes on your back. So I gave him permission to go back to my house and bring the rest of my clothing here. I am sure we can find some clothes we can fix to fit you. I even asked him to bring a few extra *kapps* and my comb and brush set."

Elizabeth's eyes widened and her heart raced. "Oh, no! You didn't let him go. That's exactly what this man will expect. He'll know we lost everything. He'll expect us to go back to the house.

He'll be watching." She started to move toward the barn. "I have to stop Thomas. He's in danger."

Mary clutched her daughter's arm and held her in place. "Thomas is a grown man. A smart man. You think he didn't think of these things, too?"

"And he still went?"

"Elizabeth, you have been gone for many years. Thomas is not the young boy you left behind. He is a strong, intelligent, hard-working, kind man. I trust him to take care of himself—and to take care of us." She looked deeply into Elizabeth's eyes. "Do you?"

Elizabeth hesitated, her mother's words hitting home. She suddenly realized she was still trying to control other people's lives. When was she going to learn that *Gott* was in charge? The only thing she could control was how she reacts to life's situations. And right now she wasn't doing a very good job.

Please, Lord, forgive me. Help me to be better. Help me to mature into the woman You have planned for me to be.

"Look." Mary gestured to the gravel lane leading to the house. "Maybe that is Thomas now."

They watched the buggy approach. As it drew nearer, both women could see Bishop Schwartz holding the reins. He circled wide and pulled to a stop with the buggy facing down the lane. Then he stepped down and fastened the reins to the rail in front of the porch.

"Is this a *gut* time to go see the sheriff? I would like to get into town and back as quickly as possible. It looks like we will soon be having snow."

All eyes searched the sky. The dark clouds on the horizon had moved closer and now hung heavily overhead, giving the sky the ominous appearance of an impending storm.

"*Kumm* inside for a few minutes and warm up, Bishop," Mary said. "I will fix you a hot cup of coffee before you go and pack another in a thermos for your trip home."

The bishop grinned. "I don't suppose it would be polite to refuse just one cup. And cookies, *ja*? You have fresh-baked cookies?"

Elizabeth laughed. "We have two different kinds to choose from. How about one of each?"

The bishop rubbed his hands together. "Lead the way. Hopefully, the snow will wait a little longer."

"When were you attacked?" the sheriff asked. He scribbled down her name, the current date and the rest Elizabeth couldn't quite make out from the angle where she was seated.

"Three days ago."

"And you've waited until now to come in?" The sheriff frowned at the bishop. "I know you folks like to handle things amongst yourselves. But don't you think this is a little bit out of your league? This isn't tipping cows or slinging eggs at houses."

"*Ja*, that is why we are here," the bishop replied.

The sheriff turned his attention to Elizabeth. He leaned back and rocked in his desk chair. "You say you got a good look at this man's face?"

"Too good a look. His hands were around my throat at the time and his face was only inches away." Elizabeth, her hands folded in her lap, sat across from the sheriff, Bishop Schwartz seated by her side.

The bishop patted Elizabeth's hand. "She has much to tell you, sheriff. It is a tale of rape. Murder. Attempted murder. Knives. Threatening notes. Burning a house to the ground."

The sheriff's mouth fell open and he stared at them in disbelief. "Nothing happens in Sunny Creek. Certainly nothing like this. And you say all of this has happened in the past three days?"

"Almost all of it," the bishop said. "Some of it may be the reason the rest has been happening." He waved at the paper beneath the sheriff's hands. "Maybe you should pay close attention and listen, sir, before you start to write. I wouldn't want you to miss anything. And I am sure you will have many questions."

The sheriff laid down his pen. He reached into his top drawer, withdrew a small tape recorder and hit the record button. "Today is Thursday, November first, and we are in my office…er, the sheriff's office in Sunny Creek, Pennsylvania, Lancaster County. This is Sheriff Tyler speaking. I am in the room with Elizabeth Lapp and Bishop Schwartz. I am about to record their statements." He pushed the recorder into the center of the desk. "State your consent to be recorded. Then whenever you're ready, Elizabeth, you can begin telling me your story."

Both Elizabeth and the bishop stated their consent.

"What brought you into my office this morning?" The sheriff leaned back in his chair. The expression on his face almost made her smile. He looked like he was hanging on to her every word. He was right. Things didn't happen in Sunny Creek. Until now.

An hour and half later the sheriff hung up his phone after speaking with the Philadelphia police and swiveled back to face them. He slid the completed recording back into the top drawer of his desk. "I am amazed at this story, Miss Lapp. I am sincerely sorry you have been going through all this." He nodded in the bishop's direction. "And I am grateful you counseled her to bring the matter to me. This is a dangerous situation and definitely not one you should be trying to handle on your own."

"Ja." The bishop acknowledged his words. "It is your job to find this man and bring him to jus-

tice. It is our job as a community to stay informed and to be vigilant and help keep one another safe."

"I understand." The sheriff wore a worried look on his face. "And the extra help from the community regarding keeping an eye out and keeping each other safe will be greatly appreciated. As you know, I only have a four-man police force plus myself. Although I will order more frequent patrols of your farms, to be honest it will be a great help to all of us if your community is made aware of the dangers and helps to monitor the area, as well."

The sheriff shifted in his chair and made direct eye contact with the bishop. "The one thing I must insist on, however, is that if you do see something or someone out of the ordinary, that you make it to a phone shanty and call it in to me. This man is dangerous and this situation is in my wheelhouse. Understand?"

Both of them nodded.

The sheriff slid a business card with his office number, cell-phone number and home number written across the back to the bishop, and then gave a second one to Elizabeth.

"I cannot stress enough the importance of avoiding contact with this man if you see him. I don't want anyone hurt or killed."

"We have no desire to confront or try to capture this criminal, Sheriff," the bishop assured him. "If we see him, we will call you. Our desire is simply to keep the members of our community informed and safe while you do your job."

"Good. Then we are in agreement." The sheriff turned his attention to Elizabeth. "The Philadelphia police are sending one of their detectives and a police sketch artist out here first thing tomorrow morning."

Elizabeth nodded. "Thank you, Sheriff."

"They weren't happy that you took off without telling them you witnessed Hannah's murder, but they sure are happy you've surfaced now. They've hit a brick wall. It was turning into a cold case. This is going to break everything wide open."

"I hope so." Elizabeth stood and the bishop joined her. "The sooner this man is behind bars, the better it will be for everyone."

"I've been sheriff of Sunny Creek for the past five years and nothing like this has ever happened here. I'm simply blown away. Let's work together as a community. I assure you we'll catch this guy. And I must confess I won't mind if it's another twenty years before I see anything like this come to our doors again." The sheriff stood and shook both their hands. "Thank you for coming in. You're doing the right thing."

"You're welcome, Sheriff," Elizabeth said. "And I'm sorry I didn't come in sooner."

"Well, you're here now and that's what counts." He tucked his thumbs into his belt. "He's got to be hiding out in someone's barn or sleeping in a field to be able to keep such a close eye on you. The last three nights have been mighty cold. I bet this guy is miserable and in a big hurry to get out of here. Snow is forecast for today. That should flush him out and when it does we'll be ready for him."

"I hope so, Sheriff. He's been pretty clever so far," Elizabeth said.

"No. No one has been looking for him. Things are about to change. Bishop Schwartz is going to put the Amish community on alert. Our local police force is going to be patrolling your farms. And help is on the way from Philadelphia. I even asked for a little extra man power besides the detective and the police sketch artist. I'd say time is no longer on this guy's side."

"Maybe he will decide to leave on his own." Even the bishop didn't look like he believed his own words.

"Or he will become more desperate, making him even more dangerous." Elizabeth shot a worried look between the two men.

"Try not to worry," the sheriff said. "Stay indoors for the rest of today if you can. Keep vigilant. And I'll see you here in my office at nine o'clock tomorrow morning. You can give your description to the police artist. We'll get it out to the media as soon as possible." He came around the desk to escort them to the door. "I don't think it will be much longer before we have this man in custody."

A sudden gust of wind blew the door open with a bang and a tall man, shaking snow from his hat, loomed on the threshold.

Instinctively the sheriff's hand flew to his gun.

"No! Relax, Sheriff. He's with me." Elizabeth laughed. "Hello, Thomas. What took you so long?"

After a quick summary of what he had missed and what the current plans would be, Thomas held open the door of the sheriff's office and accompanied Bishop Schwartz and Elizabeth outside.

"*Denki*, Thomas, for coming," the bishop said. "This snow doesn't look like it plans on stopping anytime soon."

Thomas glanced at the sky and turned up the collar of his coat.

That's an understatement if I ever heard one!

This first snow of the season looked more like a full-blown blizzard rather than a storm. The snow was blowing sideways, making visibility poor, and the cold temperature was seeping straight into his bones. If this was any indication, it was going to be a long, hard winter.

"We better get home soon. The roads are already covered with snow. The horses will find it difficult to pull a buggy through this mess if we don't get a move on."

No sooner had he spoken than a strong gust of wind blew the bishop's hat from his head and Thomas scurried to retrieve it.

"*Denki*, again." The bishop placed the hat back on. "Looks like we have accumulated two inches already. I admit I am anxious to get home."

"I saw no reason for you to have to make a third trip to my farm in one day. You have helped enough. Go home, Bishop. I will see that Elizabeth gets home safely."

The bishop climbed into his buggy. "I will stop by Levi's place and ask him to come over this evening to keep watch. He is young and sturdy. This storm won't deter him. I'll wait until after tomorrow's meeting with the police before I call a formal men's meeting and set up a schedule for the rest of us to help keep watch. I believe even this monster will seek shelter in this storm."

After watching the elderly man click the reins and pull out in the direction of his home, Thomas rechecked that the windshields on his buggy were properly fastened, then stepped up and slid onto the bench beside Elizabeth.

"I hope you will be warm enough. The wind is cold and blowing hard."

Thomas settled in. He offered a silent prayer that they would make it home safely as he often did in bad weather. He reached over and tucked a large blanket over their legs. Without further delay, he snapped the reins and pulled into the street.

"Some of the men have put propane-powered heaters in their buggies," he said as the buggy moved down Main Street. "But I am afraid to use them in such close quarters. What if a car rear-ended me?"

"I understand."

"I have looked at the heater, though. It would mount in the front, here in the middle." He pointed to a spot between them. "The tubing and propane tank would have to be in back with the *kinner*. Knowing Benjamin, that would not be safe."

"For sure." Elizabeth chuckled and adjusted the blanket. "What is this made from, Thomas? Fur does not normally weigh this much."

"I ordered it special. It is fur on both sides and has insulation within the front and back covers."

"Well, it is certainly warm." She pulled it up and covered her shoulders, too. "You don't need a heater. This is *wunderbaar.*"

He grinned. He wanted her to be comfortable and had felt bad that she might be cold.

They had traveled in a companionable silence for several miles when he shot a glance her way and asked, "What's that song I heard you singing to the *kinner* earlier this morning?"

"You heard that? I was trying to lift their spirits and calm them after the fire. I hope you don't mind."

"It was a cute song. Dashing through snow or something like that?"

Elizabeth laughed. "Something like that."

"Well, this qualifies as snow and we are definitely dashing home. Since the *kinner* are not here why don't you sing to me, Elizabeth?"

He grinned when a rosy blush colored her cheeks. She smiled coyly at him, which touched his heart. She was strong and independent, *ja*. But she was also feminine and soft and vulnerable. He liked that about her. His feelings for her were definitely not dead and gone. They'd hibernated like a bear in winter. Now that she had returned, so had his feelings, whether he wanted them to or not.

She studied him almost as if she wondered if he had been sincere when he'd asked her to sing, or if he was simply teasing her. Once she'd made up her mind, a low, pleasant hum filled the buggy and soon the words he'd heard her singing to Rachel and Benjamin followed. She had a soft, high, melodious voice. This morning he had stood in the doorway of the living room and watched his *kinner*. For once, his ever-active son sat quietly at Elizabeth's feet, playing with a wooden cow and horse while he listened to the song. His daughter, holding the plastic dog toy Elizabeth had let her keep, had sat on Elizabeth's lap. The child had barely moved and stared raptly up into her face. Apparently, she liked to listen to Elizabeth sing.

So did he.

Thomas clicked the reins and urged his mare down the street and toward the highway leading home.

ELEVEN

When the song ended, Elizabeth sang another. When she finished singing, they traveled in companionable silence. It was good having her home again.

After several minutes, he asked, "Now that you've seen the sheriff, do you feel better?"

Elizabeth nodded. "It's a load off my mind. After I help the police artist with the sketch of the suspect tomorrow, I can wash my hands of this whole mess. It won't be my responsibility anymore. I can relax and let the professionals handle things."

"It was never your responsibility."

She sighed heavily. "I know, Thomas. You want me to believe it's not my fault that a lunatic is trying to kill me and everyone close to me. I get it." She smiled at him. "But it sure feels like it's my fault. He did follow me here."

"*Ja*. And the snow is following me home. Is the snow my fault?"

Elizabeth laughed. "Point made, Thomas."

The snow grew heavier and visibility became difficult as dusk settled into darkness.

"I can see the highway up ahead. A few miles on it and we will be able to pull onto less traveled roads." Thomas wondered if he was reassuring her or himself.

Elizabeth remained burrowed beneath the blanket and quiet. He knew she was concerned about the fierceness of the storm, as well.

The sudden roar of an approaching car engine filled the air.

Both Thomas and Elizabeth looked ahead and then behind the buggy to locate the vehicle.

"Who would be crazy enough to drive his car at such a high speed in this weather?" The words tumbled from his mouth seconds before headlights of an approaching vehicle appeared on the dark country road at the top of the upcoming hill.

The mare, skittish already from the punishing storm, snorted and raised her head. The buggy swayed slightly from left to right, then back again.

"Whoa, girl. It's *allrecht*. Take it easy." Thomas tried to keep his voice calm and authoritative with the animal. The last thing he needed was his mare to break out of a trot and run freely toward the open highway. He pulled back slightly on the reins, trying to keep her in check.

The approaching car put on its bright lights and gunned the motor, picking up speed. Its tires spun a shower of snow into the air as it crested the hill. The vehicle, taking the bend in the road too quickly, slipped and slid in the freshly fallen snow.

"Thomas, be careful." Thomas could feel Elizabeth's tension as she moved closer to him, straightened her back, inhaled sharply and placed a hand on his knee. "Maybe we should pull over and let this idiot pass by."

Thomas didn't disagree, but where was there a safe place to pull over? Snowdrifts were already forming on the sides of the road and he couldn't risk the buggy getting stuck.

The car's headlights blinded them as the driver lost control and careened from his lane into theirs. The driver hit the brakes but not in time. The roaring approach of the car terrified their horse. The mare slid in the snow. The buggy swayed violently. Thomas's heartbeat kicked up several notches as he fought to keep the buggy from tilting and crashing onto the side of the road.

"Easy, girl. Take it easy."

The horse threw up her head and tried to raise up on her hind legs. Her nostrils flared and her eyes widened with fear.

The buggy tilted on two wheels.

Elizabeth let out a short scream but quickly stifled it.

Thomas banged his head on the roof. Both of them slid across the seat with the out-of-control swaying of the buggy and their bodies slammed painfully into each other.

Would he be able to stop the buggy before they hit the main intersection leading into open highway? Granted, in this weather and at this time of night traffic would be at a minimum, but it would only take one car or truck to send them careening into a ditch or worse.

Elizabeth slid her arm under his, buried her face against his sleeve and held on tight.

Thomas braced his feet against the floorboards and pulled back hard on the reins. "Whoa, girl! Stop!"

But it was too late.

The terrified horse broke into a full gallop and within seconds they burst into oncoming traffic.

The sound of someone laying on a car horn blasted so loudly Thomas thought the car was in the buggy with them. Headlights blinded them and he raised his arm to shield his eyes seconds before the car veered into the other lane, sliding and fishtailing in a deadly spin.

The signature ear-shattering blast of a semi-truck's horn sounded as its driver fought for control and with expert driving skills maneuvered his rig between the buggy and the car in his lane without striking either of them.

Thomas's horse ran into a snowdrift on the side of the road. It must have felt safer in the knee-deep snow than on the road because the buggy came to an abrupt stop and the mare stayed right where she was. A quick glance showed the truck had never paused. The car had stopped for a few minutes and then had also continued on. Thomas sat for a moment in the darkness and bowed his head.

Denki, Lord. Only You could have moved that semi out of the way.

Elizabeth had never let go of his arm. Now that they were stopped and safe, he felt her lift her head from his sleeve.

"Are you *allrecht*?" he asked.

She nodded. "Are you?"

"Ja." He held up a hand and purposely let it tremble. "A little shaken maybe, but not hurt. Think this shaking will ever go away or will I have to learn a new way to feed myself?"

Elizabeth chuckled and the tension in the cab eased for a moment. Then she looked hurriedly in every direction.

"Where is he?"

"Who?"

"You know who. This wasn't an accident. We were forced off the road. It was him."

"Not necessarily. It might have been a foolish driver going much too fast for the weather and road conditions."

She didn't look convinced and continued to stare over her shoulder. "I know it was him."

He caught and held her gaze. "I don't know who

the driver was. What I do know is *Gott* was with us. We are safe and unharmed. But we are sideways in the middle of a highway. We have to move immediately before something bad does happen."

With that said, Thomas jumped out of the cab and hurried forward to see to his mare. He stroked her and spoke to her in a calm, soothing voice. Then he grabbed her bit and led her out of the snowdrift and placed her in the right direction back onto the highway.

Hopping up on the step and back into the cab, he quickly threw the blanket over his legs. The cold chilled him to the bone. His trousers had been soaked through with snow in parts both from earlier in the storm and now from climbing through knee-high snow to reach his horse. His body shuddered.

He didn't think the driver had been Hannah's killer. The man might be desperate but Thomas didn't believe he was stupid. If it had been him, he had ample opportunity to slam into their buggy and finish off both of them and he hadn't.

No.

Most likely it had been an inexperienced driver going much too fast on unfamiliar roads in inclement weather.

However, it didn't change how terrifying the incident had been.

Thomas refused to allow Elizabeth to see how

badly it had shaken him. He'd rather she believe it was the weather that caused his trembling.

He shot her a reassuring grin.

"Homeward bound. I could use some time in front of a roaring fire with a hot cup of coffee." He winked at her. "And one of your homemade cookies for sure."

Thomas clicked the reins.

Mary approached carrying two mugs. "Mind if I sit with you? I brought both of us some hot tea."

Elizabeth accepted the mug. "*Denki*. Of course I'd enjoy your company." She gestured to the rocking chair beside her. "Sit with me."

"You've been very quiet lately, spending most of your evenings sitting on this porch until everyone else has long gone to bed."

Elizabeth sipped her tea and then tossed her mother a smile. "Is there a question in there someplace?"

"No questions. Observations."

Elizabeth continued to drink her tea.

"It's been two weeks since you met with the police artist. Thomas tells me there is still no news from Philadelphia, no new leads or clues to Hannah's killer."

"True. The last I heard they were unable to find her mother's journals. They must have been in the box I dropped when I ran from the condo and that criminal probably found them. Without those journals the police have been unable to discover the man's name or confirm the story I told them of Hannah's conception. So they're right back where they started. No leads. No clues. Nothing."

"They have the picture they made from your description."

Elizabeth shrugged. "It hasn't done much good. The sheriff told me the Philadelphia police gave it to the media. They also made flyers and hung them in bus stops, airports, rail stations, post offices and other crowded areas, but nothing of substance came from them.

"I'm not surprised, though." She looked at her mother. "I tried, *Mamm*. I did my best to work with the artist. But the composite drawing... I don't know. It resembled him in some ways, but something was off and I couldn't put my finger on it. Yes, it looked like the man. But do I think it was a close enough replication of him to be easily recognized? No. I don't. It was too generic. The likeness could have been one of a hundred men. Maybe that's why the police didn't get any viable calls."

"You did your best. That is all anyone can expect of you."

"It wasn't enough."

"Elizabeth, your best is always enough."

"But he's still out there somewhere."

Mary reached over and patted her hand. "It's been more than two weeks since anyone has seen or heard anything out of the ordinary. For whatever reason, I think the man decided to leave. I believe we are safe now."

Elizabeth chewed on her lower lip. "As long as he is free and not behind bars we will never be safe."

"Time will tell, child. But Thomas agrees with me. Even the bishop thinks we are safe. The men in the community are no longer taking shifts through the night keeping watch. He released them yesterday. He feels something more would have happened by now if the man was still here."

"I agree. I think he left, too. I'm just not sure why he would. He's a desperate man and I did not give him what he was looking for. It doesn't make sense to me that he would leave." She sighed. "On the other hand, I can't see him hiding out in people's barns or sleeping in the fields for this amount of time. In town the inns have his picture and the sheriff told them to notify him immediately if this guy shows up. So, yes, I think he left. But that doesn't mean he won't come back… and probably when we've let our guard down and least expect it."

Mary scolded her. "Is this what you plan to do? Spend the rest of your life keeping guard at night? Being afraid? Looking over your shoulder? That is not life, Elizabeth."

She stamped her foot on the porch floor to gain Elizabeth's full attention. "You are letting him win, *ja*? You are so afraid he will steal your life you don't see that he already has and you are continuing to let him do it." She waited until they made eye contact. "Elizabeth, listen to me, please. Life is short. Don't make it shorter. Be grateful to *Gott* that you have today—for that is all we are promised, *ja*? Make the most of your life. I fear you have already missed so much."

Mary pointed to the sky. "Look at those stars! Aren't they beautiful? *Gott* placed each and every one of them in their own special spot. He has planned for our special spot in this life, too." She smiled. "Daughter, I want the best for you. Enjoy the sun on your face. Laugh with the *kinner*. Work hard and enjoy the fruits of your labor in a fine feast you've prepared for the church service, or a quilt you made and put in your hope chest. Help others who are not as fortunate as yourself. There are many people who need an extra hand or are alone and lonely."

Mary leaned forward in her rocker and drilled her point home. "Live your life, Elizabeth, with gratitude and joy and a serving heart. Do that and I am sure *Gott* will bless you with peace and happiness."

"Sometimes, *Mamm*, that is not so easy to do." Elizabeth stared up at the sky. "But you're right about those stars. It is, indeed, a beautiful sight."

"Don't waste the time *Gott* has given you. It will be over all too soon."

Elizabeth frowned and studied her mother more closely. "Are you all right, *Mamm*? Your health, I mean. Are you well?"

Mary laughed. "What? You think I am dying because I am trying to encourage you to live?" She shook her head. "I am fine. But it hurts my heart to watch you nervous and fearful and spending your nights alone staring into the darkness."

"You're right. It's time I allow the police to worry about this criminal," Elizabeth said. "And past time to turn the entire situation over to *Gott*."

"Gut." Mary smiled widely.

They spent the next hour talking in generalities about the latest antics of the *kinner*, the weather, even who was going to make what dish for the upcoming Thanksgiving feast only a couple of weeks away. It was time to move inside when her mother pinned her with another question.

"I feel there is more on your mind than this evil man who no longer seems to be a threat to us. We said no more secrets. What else is bothering you?"

Elizabeth sighed heavily. Her mother didn't miss much as far as she was concerned, never had. She folded her hands in her lap and forced herself to say the words she hadn't even wanted to think about.

"It's time we leave, *Mamm*."

"Leave? Thomas has not said anything like that to me. Has he mentioned it to you?"

"No, of course not. He is too kind to ask us to

go. But we cannot continue to live in his home. This is his home, *Mamm*. His *kinner*. His family. Not ours."

Mary nodded. "This is true." She slowly pushed the rocker with her toe. "It's just been *wunderbaar* to be a part of a family again." Her voice sounded wistful. She glanced over at Elizabeth. "I have been lonely sometimes without you and your father in the house. And, I must admit, I enjoy the *kinner*."

Mary stood and picked up the empty mugs.

"But you are right. This is not our family. It is time to go home. We will leave in the morning."

Before her mother turned and went inside, Elizabeth thought she'd seen tears glistening in her mother's eyes—or were they her own?

TWELVE

Thomas stood at the far end by the tack room and was washing up in the sink. His eyes lit on Elizabeth the moment she stepped inside the barn.

"*Guder mariye*, Thomas."

"*Guder mariye*, Elizabeth."

"Breakfast is ready when you are."

He turned to face her and wiped his hands on a towel. "I am always ready for one of your meals. You and Mary spoil me." He patted his stomach. "I am getting fat."

Elizabeth laughed and the sound of it sent a warmth through him. "Then I'll have to find more chores to burn off the extra calories because I made cinnamon rolls especially for you today."

"Cinnamon rolls!" He placed his hands on his heart. "*Denki*. You have made my day." He crossed the barn floor and followed her into the house.

He wondered if it had been as difficult on her as it had been on him since she'd moved back to her mother's house almost two weeks ago. He knew she'd been happy in his home and he'd done everything he could to make her feel welcome. And the *kinner* missed her.

He had brought the *kinner* to visit a couple of times each week when he came to do the heavier chores for her mother.

But it wasn't the same.

He had to admit he had enjoyed seeing her at every meal. Sitting with her in the evenings on the porch. Playing together with the *kinner*.

It had been easy to pretend they were a family. It had felt *gut* to be a family again. And it had been devastatingly hard to acknowledge that they weren't family and it was time for her to leave.

Thomas hung his hat on the peg by the door and slipped past her into the kitchen.

"*Guder mariye*, Mary. Something smells good."

Her mother smiled. "You say that every morning, Thomas."

"And I mean it every morning, Mary."

They both laughed and he pulled out the chair at the head of the table and sat down.

"*Kumm*, Elizabeth, before it gets cold." Thomas beckoned her over his shoulder. "I am not going to be polite this morning. I will claim all the bacon if you don't fill your plate before I do." He pulled out the chair beside him, then turned his attention back to Mary.

"Rebecca asked me to remind you to make your egg custard for Thanksgiving dinner tomorrow. It is one of her favorites."

Elizabeth sat in the chair beside him.

He grinned at her and wiggled his eyebrows. "And I would not mind if you make your green-bean casserole. Your *daed* and I used to challenge each other for the last scoop."

"I remember."

Her smile seemed bittersweet and Thomas wondered if she was thinking of her father and missing him. Probably missing Hannah, too. He sensed a bit of loneliness in the wistfulness of her voice. He'd caught that same longing in Mary's voice a time or two over the years.

He reached into his trouser pocket and extended his hand toward Mary. "And I was asked to deliver this to you. It was included in a package I received from my parents."

He held out a letter.

Mary took it and quickly shoved it into her apron pocket.

"Mamm?" Elizabeth seemed surprised and shot her a questioning look.

"What?" The woman tried to evade Elizabeth's penetrating stare. "It's simply a letter from a friend."

Thomas grinned at the telltale blush in Mary's

cheeks and almost laughed out loud at the astonished look on Elizabeth's face.

"A male friend?" Elizabeth's words were a whisper.

"His name is Joshua. He is a widower. He lost his wife the same year I lost your father. He goes to Sarasota every winter along with Thomas's parents."

"Have I ever met him?"

"*Neh.* I think he and his wife moved here the year after you left."

"Why haven't you mentioned him to me before?" Elizabeth grinned.

Mary sent a censuring look her way. "What's there to mention? We are simply friends. It is nothing you need to concern yourself with."

But Mary's blush deepened and she couldn't seem to make eye contact with either one of them. She quickly changed the subject.

"Thomas, Elizabeth and I need to go to town later today. Do you have time to take us?"

"*Mamm!* Thomas does enough for us. I am perfectly capable of driving the buggy into town."

Thomas ignored Elizabeth's outburst. "I will be happy to take the two of you. I'll come back right after lunch to pick you up."

"Thomas, I can drive a buggy…"

There she goes again. Hands on hips. Eyes flashing. Heels dug in and ready for a fight. Boy, he had missed her. She's as ornery as an old mule at times.

"Don't get your feathers in an uproar. I know you can drive a buggy. And you can muck a stall and feed chickens and milk cows." He placed his hand over hers on the table. "But it doesn't mean you have to. You have a man more than willing and able to do it for you." He removed his hand, lifted his mug and took a swig of coffee. "Besides, I was hoping you and your mother would help me in return."

Elizabeth looked at him suspiciously. "What do you need from us?"

"Both of the *kinner* need new boots. I am not good with shopping unless it is for farm supplies or something I need for the horses. I was hoping you would help me with that chore."

"We'd love to help," Mary said before Elizabeth could open her mouth.

"*Gut*, it's settled." He stood and headed for the door before Elizabeth could protest some more. "Be back around one."

He slipped outside, skipped down the steps and found himself humming as he climbed into his buggy to head home and do his own chores.

He loved getting Elizabeth all riled up. It was fun.

He loved the glint in her eyes, her stubbornness, her determination to prove she was as good as any man…or any*one* for that matter.

He loved her strength and independence.

He loved…

Shock raced through his body as he realized the direction his thoughts had gone and he immediately made himself think about something else.

"Watch me, Miss Elizabeth. Watch how fast I can run in my new boots." Benjamin ran across the front porch of the general store with his little sister skipping right behind him.

"Don't go too far," Elizabeth called. "I want both of you to stay with me."

They turned and raced back again, the sound of their boots clomping across the wooden planks.

Benjamin pulled to a stop in front of her. "Aren't these boots fast?"

Elizabeth smiled. He was such an adorable little imp. "*Ja*, Benjamin. I think you picked out the fastest boots in the entire store."

"I have boots, too." Rachel held up one foot.

"*Ja*, sweetie. You have new boots, too." Elizabeth reached out for the girl's hand, but before she could clasp it, the child pulled away, let out a cry and started running away.

"Rachel, stop." She moved quickly and fastened her hold on the girl's shoulders. "Where are you going? We have to stay here and wait for your *daed*."

Rachel pointed and started to whine. "Doggy!"

Elizabeth's gaze went in the direction the child

pointed. She had dropped the little plastic toy and it had rolled off the porch and was lying in the street.

"You wait right here! Don't move." She hurried down and snatched up the toy only moments before she heard the clumping of hooves behind her and knew Thomas's buggy was right behind her. She ran to the steps, grabbed the edge of her skirt and hopped onto the planking. She grinned when Rachel clasped the dog to her chest. She really loved that little plastic toy.

"Here, let's put it in your pocket until we get home." She slid it into the pocket of Rachel's apron. "It's time for the doggy to take a nap. He'll be safe in your pocket and you can play with him when you get home."

Rachel grinned and patted her pocket. "Night, night, doggy."

"*Daed*, look at my new boots. They're the fastest boots in the store." Benjamin took off again, running back and forth across the porch, skirting customers and making zooming noises as he rushed by.

Thomas grabbed him on his second pass. "Whoa, partner. You're a little too fast. You don't want to get in the way of the store's customers, do you?"

The boy looked at the other adults milling in and out of the store as if it was the first time he'd even noticed them.

"When we get home," his father said, "you can run as fast and as much as you want on our front porch. How's that?"

"Yippee." Benjamin jumped up and down. "Can we go home now, *Daed*?"

"I don't know. Can we?" Thomas looked their way. "Are you ladies finished with your shopping?"

"Almost, Thomas," Mary replied. "I forgot to buy a spice I need."

"I could use some new material for a dress, too. I didn't have a chance to look while I was watching the *kinner*," Elizabeth added.

"Sounds to me like the ladies need some lady shopping time." He hoisted Rachel up on his shoulders and grabbed Benjamin's hand. "Why don't the three of us go over to Millie's café and get some hot chocolate with whipped cream. What do you say?"

The kids cheered.

"That settles it, then. You ladies enjoy your shopping. Take your time. We'll be right across the street. Come join us when you're done."

Elizabeth thanked him and watched them cross the street and disappear inside the café.

"He's a good *daed*. Those *kinner* are blessed," Mary said.

Elizabeth agreed.

"You still haven't told him your secret even though you said you would. Why?"

"I will, *Mamm*. I'm not trying to keep it a secret anymore. Honestly, I'm not. But after we moved home…well, there hasn't been an opportunity. What am I supposed to do? Follow him out to the barn and drop the news on him while he's milking the cows?" She locked eyes with her mother. "You know I haven't had any alone time with him since we moved back. This is a sensitive and personal subject. The timing has to be right."

Her *mamm*'s lips twisted in a wry grin. "Thanksgiving is in two days. I am sure you will be able to find a few minutes to talk with him privately. And I am equally sure you will both be grateful that you did."

Elizabeth put her arm around her mother's shoulders and steered her toward the store. "Okay. You're right. No more excuses. I'll pull him aside and tell him right after the Thanksgiving meal."

"Gut."

They were almost to the store entrance when Elizabeth froze. She couldn't move a muscle if her life depended upon it. Her breathing quickened and a sick tightening grasped her chest. Despite the winter weather a bead of sweat broke out on her forehead and the pulse at her temples throbbed.

Calm down. You're having a panic attack. That's all it is.

Unfortunately her body didn't want to listen to

her mind. The blood drained out of her face and her knees wobbled.

Stop this before it gets worse. Inhale sharply and exhale slowly. C'mon, you can do it.

"Elizabeth, what is it? What's wrong?"

She closed her eyes, took a deep breath, pursed her lips and exhaled as slowly as she could.

"Elizabeth, answer me. What's wrong? You're scaring me."

She took another calming breath, opened her eyes and looked at her mother. "It's him."

"Who?" Her mother tossed looks in every direction.

"The killer." Her words were a mere whisper.

Mary grabbed her arm and held on tight. "Where, child? Where is he? We need to run and get Thomas."

Mary started to pull her toward the steps but Elizabeth stood her ground. "No, *Mamm*. He's not here in person. That's his picture."

She pointed to a newspaper in a display rack near the entrance of the general store. She didn't know how she'd missed it earlier. She'd probably been so busy paying attention to the children that she didn't notice her surroundings.

Mary stepped forward and peered at the paper behind the glass.

The headline read, The President Arrives in Philadelphia.

"The president?" Mary's voice quavered and

she looked at her daughter as though she had lost her mind.

"No, *Mamm*. Of course not." Elizabeth jabbed the glass with her index finger. "Him. The man in the background."

"Which one? There are several men standing behind him."

"The one on the end of the podium standing by the flag."

Elizabeth rummaged in her purse to find enough change to purchase the paper. When she did, she opened the glass covering and pulled out the newspaper. With trembling hands, she held it up for a closer look.

Her mother peered over her arm. "Who is he? Does it tell you his name?"

Elizabeth scanned the caption. "Oh, dear heavenly Father, help us. No wonder he was so desperate not to be identified."

"Why? Who is he?" Her mother pulled on her arm and tried to read the paper herself.

Elizabeth gave a long, heavy sigh. "His name is Richard Dolan. He's a Pennsylvania senator."

"Senator? That can't be, can it?" Mary grabbed her daughter's arm and forced Elizabeth to look at her. "You're telling me a senator may have raped my best friend and killed his own daughter?"

The anguish Elizabeth saw in her mother's face made her realize she wasn't the only one who had lost a dear friend or others she'd cared about. She wasn't the only one hurting and afraid.

"Well, obviously he wouldn't have been a senator all those years ago, but he is now."

"Are you certain it's him?"

"I wish I wasn't, *Mamm*. But this is the man who killed Hannah. Now we know why he left. He only had a couple of weeks to return home, make things appear normal and prepare for his arrangements to be with the president in Philadelphia for this big fund-raiser. He couldn't be missing in action. He had to go home."

Her hands shook and she almost dropped the paper.

"Once the president has returned to Washington, Senator Dolan is free to come and go as he pleases." She shot a glance at her mother and knew she couldn't hide her terror. "He's coming back, *Mamm*. I know he is."

"Don't panic. At least we'll be prepared this time. We'll tell Thomas and the bishop what we know and what we suspect."

"*Ja*, but first I have to tell the sheriff." She faced her mother and clasped her forearms. "I need you to go across the street and tell Thomas what's happened and where I am." Elizabeth stepped back and clutched the paper against her chest. "This newspaper went to press last night in order to be on the stands today. We have to hurry. Dolan could already be here."

THIRTEEN

"Ms. Lapp, come in." The sheriff stood and came around his desk as Elizabeth stomped the snow from her boots on the doormat. The heat in the room was a welcome change from the frigid temperatures outside and the smell of fresh coffee almost made her drool.

"Please, have a seat. I planned to drive out later today to talk to you. You've just saved me the trip."

Elizabeth strode into the room and stood in front of the sheriff. "You were coming to see me? Why? Did they catch him?"

"Please." He pulled out the chair. "Sit down."

She did as he requested.

The sheriff went back behind his desk, sat in his well-worn brown leather chair and folded his hands on his desk.

"May I offer you a cup of coffee?"

"No, *denki*." As much as she'd love to take him up on the offer, this wasn't a social call and she couldn't help feeling the sheriff was stalling for some reason.

"Did you find him?" Elizabeth asked again.

"No. Not yet."

"Then why were you coming to see me?"

"The Philadelphia police called and…uh, asked me to speak with you."

He squirmed in his chair, the leather squeaking beneath his excess weight. He fumbled with a pencil on his desk and seemed to be having difficulty making eye contact with her.

"There's no easy way to tell you…"

"Yes there is, Sheriff. Say it straight out. I've lived in your world for the past seven years. There isn't much that surprises me anymore."

He studied her face and gave a curt nod. "Very well. The Philadelphia police gave a press conference earlier today. They announced that they believe they have a witness to the murder who has just agreed to come forward with physical evidence identifying Hannah Fischer's killer. If the information is viable, they expect to be able to make an arrest shortly."

"What?" Elizabeth fell back in her chair and her mouth gaped open. "I never agreed to any such thing."

"We know. It's a ploy. That's why I was coming out to your place. They want me to pick you up and put you in protective custody for a few weeks so that you won't be in the line of fire when the killer returns and tries to silence you."

"A ploy?" Elizabeth couldn't contain her shock. She leaned her forearms against the desktop. "Let me get this straight. You were coming out to my home to snatch me up a day and a half before Thanksgiving to hide me away because the Philadelphia police decided to use me as bait."

His neck colored and he squirmed even more.

"They're hoping the fish will come after the bait only to find an empty hook. Is that what you're doing?"

"Not me, Ms. Lapp. The higher-ups made that decision." He cleared his throat. "I understand why you're upset. I'd be, too, if someone dangled me on the end of a fishing line to catch a killer. Particularly without my knowledge or permission." He sat back in his seat.

"But what can I say? You're all we've got. The composite drawing didn't help. You are the only witness to the crime. All roads turned stone-cold. They thought this would flush him out."

"I'm sure it will." Elizabeth didn't know whether to be furious or grateful that law enforcement was so invested in solving the case.

The sheriff's mouth twisted. "Truthfully, I agree with them." He held his palms out to prevent her from protesting. "Not that I like the way they did it. Not telling you or anything. But it probably will make him show up in Sunny Creek again.

Soon. That's why I can't let you leave my office today. I've got to put you in protective custody."

Before Elizabeth could protest, Thomas opened the door. He removed his hat as he entered, nodded to the sheriff and pulled out the chair beside Elizabeth.

"Are you *allrecht*?" he asked her. "Mary just told me."

"I'm fine, Thomas." She glared at the man sitting across from her. "Aren't I, Sheriff?"

Thomas shot a quizzical look at both Elizabeth and the sheriff but remained quiet.

"Law enforcement decided to take matters into their own hands." Although she spoke to Thomas, she never took her eyes from the sheriff. "They decided to use me as bait—without my knowledge or permission, of course."

"What do you mean 'bait'?"

The sheriff quickly brought Thomas up to speed on what had happened. "So we're going to take her into protective custody for a week or two and see what happens."

Both of them spoke simultaneously.

"*Neh*. You can't do that," Thomas said.

"I am not staying in protective custody," Elizabeth said.

The sheriff sighed. "Look…"

"No, Sheriff. You look. I came here today for a reason." Elizabeth leaned back in her chair. "I am about to break this case wide open for you. I know the name of the killer and where you can find him." She smiled at the astonished look on the man's face.

The sheriff looked from one to the other, then settled his gaze on Elizabeth.

"Maybe you should tell me what evidence you have. Then we'll discuss the custody situation."

Elizabeth placed the newspaper on the sheriff's desk and jabbed her index finger on the picture of the man standing on the platform. "That is the man you're looking for, Sheriff. His name is Richard Dolan."

The sheriff picked up the paper, looked at the picture and laughed.

"That's funny, Ms. Lapp. Guess you're entitled to at least one joke after what we're asking of you."

The sheriff's grin dissipated when he realized that neither Thomas nor Elizabeth were laughing with him.

"Wait a minute." He tossed the paper back onto the desk. "You're serious? You're trying to tell me that Richard Dolan—Senator Richard Dolan— is the man who attacked you in the barn? That this man—" he shook the edges of the newspaper "—killed Hannah Fischer."

"That's exactly what she's saying, Sheriff." Thomas stared hard at the man, almost daring him to contradict Elizabeth.

The grin, although a weak one, was back on the sheriff's face. He glanced back and forth between them then turned his attention to Elizabeth.

"Ms. Lapp, I am sure you *think* this is your culprit, but I assure you that you're wrong."

"Really? Tell me, Sheriff, was it you who got a good look at his face while he was trying to choke you to death? Or was it me?"

The sheriff shook his head, apparently having great difficulty wrapping his mind around her words. "Ms. Lapp, this man has built his entire political career based on family values. It's even rumored he's going to run for president in the next election."

"Well, that certainly sounds like motive to me." Elizabeth folded her hands in her lap and stared him down.

The sheriff's disbelief of Elizabeth's words irritated Thomas and he couldn't keep silent any longer. "Elizabeth would never lie to you about this. If she says this is the man, I believe her."

Elizabeth smiled at him.

The sheriff rummaged in his file drawer and withdrew a copy of the composite picture. He placed the newspaper and the drawing side by side and spun them around to face them.

"I'll admit that there are some similarities. I'll give you that. But there's no way the man in this picture is the same man in the newspaper."

Thomas slid the pictures closer to Elizabeth. "What do you think?"

"I agree with the sheriff. That's why we didn't get any leads when the media ran with it. The drawing isn't accurate." She studied them for a few minutes, then looked up at him with a grin. "I knew something was wrong with this drawing, Thomas, but I couldn't put my finger on what it was."

Excitement sounded in her voice. "Look!" She jabbed her index finger on the papers and then locked her gaze with the sheriff's. "The chin is different. So are the eyes. This drawing is too generic. It could fit the description of a multitude of men. That's why no one recognized him." She slid the papers back. "But Senator Richard Dolan is the man who killed Hannah. He is the same man who tried to choke me to death." She sat back and stared at him. "Now I want to know what you intend to do about it."

The sheriff released a slow, heavy sigh. "Ms. Lapp, do you have any idea what the Philadelphia police are going to do when I call them? They're going to laugh me right out of my job."

"Why's that, Sheriff?" Thomas asked. "Don't you think powerful people can be bad people?" He leaned forward to emphasize his point. "Do you know your Bible, sir? There are many leaders in the Bible who did terrible, evil things. Some killed two-year-old babies. Others ordered the murder of Christ, *Gott*'s *sohn*. Is this senator more important than any of those men?

The sheriff ran a hand across his balding scalp. "Okay, I'll make the call. I just can't promise they'll take her seriously." He turned his attention to Elizabeth. "Now what's this about not staying here in protective custody?"

"The day after tomorrow is Thanksgiving. I intend to spend the day with my family and friends."

"I can't keep you safe if you're walking around out there, Ms. Lapp. I think I'd skip Thanksgiving dinner this year in return for being alive to eat it next year."

"You don't understand."

"Enlighten me."

"I have no doubt you will keep me safe if I follow your plan and let you stash me someplace under armed guard." Elizabeth stood and pointed, again, to the man in the picture. "And what do you think this man will do if he can't get to me?" She squared her shoulders and looked him right in the eye. "He will be furious. He will seek revenge on me and he will hurt the people I care about, the people he can get near. I refuse to let that happen."

"If you walk out those doors, I can't promise I can keep you safe."

"I understand. But I know you'll try. And I know the Philadelphia police are on their way and they intend to help catch Mr. Dolan. The rest is in *Gott*'s hands and that's good enough for me."

"Ms. Lapp, I don't think you fully understand the danger you are in, particularly after today's press conference. If you are correct and our culprit is Mr. Dolan, then he will stop at nothing to get to you. You threaten his current career and any aspirations for a higher one."

"Has anyone considered picking up Mr. Dolan for custody now before he comes to Sunny Creek?" Thomas asked. "Seems to me prevention is better than hoping for a cure. Get the man. Lock him up. Problem solved."

The sheriff grimaced. "I wish it could be that easy. I'll call the Philadelphia police in just a minute. But I'm more worried about the timing. If Ms. Lapp is correct about Mr. Dolan, then he isn't sitting around waiting for us to knock on his door. He's making a beeline for Sunny Creek to shut her up before she can bring him down."

Worry and fear tore at Thomas's gut. What if he couldn't keep her safe? He clasped her hand. "Elizabeth, maybe I was wrong. Maybe you should consider going into this protective custody the sheriff is talking about."

"*Neh*, Thomas." She patted his hand and then spoke directly to the sheriff.

"If you want to use me as bait, then use me. I

intend to stay right out in the open, where he can easily find me. I will not allow him to hurt any of the people I love. I'm done with running away." She smiled at Thomas and her voice softened. "I've learned that running away never solves anything."

Thomas took a moment to let her words register and then grinned when he realized her words had a deeper, personal meaning.

She returned the grin then faced the sheriff.

"No, Sheriff. I'm not hiding. I'm not running. This has to end. I want my life back and the lives of the people in my community to return to normal. This man has stolen enough from us. I won't let him steal anything more."

Thomas stood and placed his hand lightly on her shoulder. "We will protect her, Sheriff. That is our job." He put his hat back on his head. "It is your job to catch this man. We hope you will do your job…soon."

Without another word, they turned and walked out of the sheriff's office.

Thomas drew her close as they walked down the street to the café, where Mary and the *kinner* waited. She smiled at him and did her best to look unaffected but he could feel an occasional shudder and he didn't believe it was from the cold.

She seemed skittish at every sudden sound and wary of every approaching man on the street.

He almost wished he could turn her around,

march her back into the sheriff's office and call the whole thing off. But he knew she was doing the right thing. The brave thing. It had to be done. It was time for this terrorizing to end.

He lowered his head and said a silent prayer while they walked.

Heavenly Father, give me the courage and strength and wisdom to face the battle ahead beside her. Help me keep her safe.

They had reached the café when Thomas caught her arm and stopped her from entering. Surprised, she turned and looked at him.

"It is normal to be afraid, Elizabeth." He smiled down at her. "We will be afraid together. No matter what happens, this terrible situation has to end. Now. *Ja?*"

"*Ja*, Thomas."

"And you will not have to face this man alone. I will be by your side. And we will have extra help from the men in our community, too."

She reached up and caressed his face. "*Denki*, Thomas."

"Remember, Elizabeth, he is just a man, not a giant or a monster. Men make mistakes. This man will make one and the sheriff will arrest him."

Elizabeth smiled. "Even if he is a giant, Thomas, we know how to handle that, don't we? David slew the giant, Goliath, with a slingshot and a stone." She clasped his hand, pulled him toward the door to the café and tossed a question over her shoulder. "By the way, Thomas, do you happen to know where I can buy a slingshot?"

FOURTEEN

Thanksgiving dawned clear, crisp and cold. The remaining snow from the last storm had formed ice crystals that glistened in the sun's morning rays. The temperature had risen slightly. It would be a good day to bundle up the *kinner* to play outside. Maybe they could go sledding. Her mother's field had undulating small hills that would be perfect for it.

Elizabeth crossed to the barn to bring in some mason jars of corn and green beans for the dinner preparation. She startled and almost dropped them when she turned and saw the sheriff standing by the barn door.

He removed his hat. "Sorry to scare you, Ms. Lapp. I thought you'd heard me pull up."

"That's all right, Sheriff. I startle easily these days. How can I help you?"

The sheriff had stopped by twice in the past day and a half and a patrol car had come by at least four times. Today's visit was the first time he had actually stopped to talk. Something must be up.

"I thought I'd stop and bring you up-to-date on the investigation."

"I'd appreciate that."

He told her that the Philadelphia police had reacted as he had initially said they would. But after a series of jokes and jibes, when they realized he was serious, they got to work. They went to the senator's Pennsylvania residence to speak with him and were told by his wife that he had flown to Washington on business. A check of the airlines proved that was untrue.

They did not question his wife about his whereabouts on the day of Hannah Fischer's murder, or the attempts on Elizabeth's life, because they didn't want to tip their hand that he was being investigated just yet.

They were unable to get current contact information from his office assistant other than his personal cell-phone number. She didn't seem to be aware of any business appointments in Washington. The assistant assumed the appointments must be of a personal nature.

The police hit pay dirt, though, with further questioning. The senator's assistant had recognized a picture they showed her of Hannah. Upon further questioning, she remembered the young woman had been in the office. She checked the calendar and confirmed that Hannah had had an appointment with the senator a month before her death. The assistant didn't know what they'd discussed, but she remembered that there had been an argument between the senator and the woman. She'd heard raised voices coming from his office, but had been unable to make out any of the words. The young woman stormed out of the senator's office appearing angry and upset. The senator had slammed his office door. He'd never confided in his assistant about what the young woman wanted or what the argument had been about. He dismissed her questions and nothing else ever came of the encounter.

The police weren't laughing anymore. Senator Richard Dolan had suddenly become the number-one person of interest in this case.

Elizabeth took a deep breath and processed the new information. She nodded. "Thank you, Sheriff. I appreciate the update."

The sheriff donned his hat. "Happy to do it."

"I guess things will start moving pretty quickly now," Elizabeth said. "Either the law will locate him and bring him in for questioning, or he will show up here and attempt to finish what he started."

The sheriff frowned. "That's about the size of it, Miss Lapp. Are you sure you don't want to take me up on that offer of protective custody?"

Of course I do. I want to hole up somewhere and stay safe until this whole mess is over.

Every bone in her body shivered with fear. But she knew she couldn't do it. She couldn't leave her community exposed to a madman who was looking for her.

"Thank you, Sheriff. I'll be fine."

He nodded. "Well, you'll see a few extra people around. We have undercover agents posing as your mail carrier, your milkman and an extra unmarked car making a patrol round or two, so don't get skittish if you don't see the regular people."

"Thanks, again. I appreciate the heads-up."

She watched him turn to leave and started toward the house when Thomas appeared in his wake. "Are you *allrecht*? What did the sheriff want?"

Elizabeth smiled. Thomas, true to his word, had been like her shadow ever since they'd left the sheriff's office the day before yesterday. He tried to stay out of her way as she went about her day, but she was well aware that he was always close by. And when he had to leave, he made sure one of the other men in their community dogged her every step.

Elizabeth had to laugh. She wasn't sure whether the men were more afraid of the elusive villain or of Thomas's wrath if they let her out of their sight.

"I can't stay out here in the barn talking. I have to get started on that green-bean casserole you like so much if I hope to have it ready for our

Thanksgiving dinner. Our guests will be arriving before you know it."

"Elizabeth, I need to know…"

"*Ja*, I know, Thomas. *Kumm* inside with me. *Mamm* is going to want to know what the sheriff said, too. I'll fill you both in over a hot cup of coffee."

True to her word, Elizabeth updated them on the sheriff's visit. They tossed worried looks at each other but neither said anything negative to Elizabeth. Nevertheless an uneasy expectancy settled over the room. He was coming. The three of them knew it and there was little anyone could do about it.

At Mary's suggestion, they clasped hands and prayed.

The rest of the morning passed in a hurried blur of cooking, cleaning and more cooking.

Thomas played outside in the snow with the *kinner* but Elizabeth noticed how he stayed even closer to the house since the sheriff's news.

By midafternoon buggies filled the yard as the other families began to arrive. The sound of *kinner*'s laughter and high-pitched voices filled the air as games of tag and softball ensued. The women gathered in the kitchen. Many had brought casseroles or homemade bread. Several women brought fresh-baked pies. The men worked together to move aside the living-room furniture and set up multiple long tables and benches, while Bishop Schwartz claimed the chore of starting a fire in the fireplace and keeping it stoked.

The meal came together in perfect harmony. The aromas of fresh breads, roasted chicken, stuffing, vegetable casseroles and a variety of pies caused more than one stomach to rumble and everyone to sniff the air with pleasure.

While they all ate to the point of overeating, the room buzzed with robust conversations. The men could be heard talking about spring crops, weather predictions and even Lucah's problem with a lame horse. The women spoke of new quilting patterns, recipes and Agnes Hofsteadter's upcoming baby shower.

No one mentioned the subject that Elizabeth was sure wore on everyone's minds, and she was grateful. It gave her the opportunity to relax for a little while. She joined the various conversations, filled her plate more than once, laughed at a child's antics and thanked *Gott* multiple times that she had finally come home again.

When the meal ended and everyone scattered to help clean up, Elizabeth slipped up beside Thomas. He was getting ready to help carry a bench out to the waiting buggy.

Surreptitiously, Elizabeth grabbed his sleeve and held him in place. Lowering her voice to a mere whisper, she asked, "Thomas, do you think when you're finished that you and I could take a walk for a few minutes. I have something important I need to discuss with you."

His brow wrinkled in concern. "Is everything *allrecht*?"

"*Ja*, no worries." She smiled confidently at him even though her pulse raced like a thoroughbred's at the opening shot. "I have something I need to say that is best said in private."

His concerned, puzzled look didn't go away, but he nodded.

Elizabeth turned the corner and stood for a second leaning against the hall wall.

Now or never, Elizabeth. No more secrets. You can do this.

She took a deep breath and exhaled long and hard.

Please, Lord, give him the grace to forgive me.

As if today wasn't stressful enough, she had told her mother she would be open and honest with Thomas.

A killer on the loose with her in his crosshairs. Long-buried secrets about to be exposed. Today couldn't get much better.

Elizabeth's shoulders stooped as if she carried the weight of the world on them. Oh, well. She'd find out soon enough if this day would, indeed, be one to be thankful for. She pushed off from the wall and headed into the kitchen to help the women clean up.

* * *

"Will you be home before I go to bed? I want you to say my night prayers with me."

"I don't know, *sohn*. It is already getting late and there is still much for me to do here." Thomas ruffled Benjamin's hair. "Did you have a *gut* time today?"

"It was *wunderbaar, Daed*. I hit two of the balls Levi threw to me. I tagged Henry and John and Micah. And Miss Mary let me have an extra piece of apple pie." He rubbed his small, rotund belly. "I am full up." His grin barely fit his face and his eyes shone with excitement. "She even gave me a scoop of vanilla ice cream on my second piece of pie."

Thomas laughed loudly. "Well, let's hope, *sohn*, that your belly doesn't protest later tonight that you shoved too many goodies into it."

Rachel sat on Rebecca's lap in the buggy with Benjamin tucked in beside her, and Thomas pressed a kiss onto his daughter's forehead. Clasping both of his children's hands, he said, "Why don't we say a prayer together now just in case I can't get home before bedtime."

The children joined him in prayer, then gave him hugs and multiple kisses before he stepped away from the buggy. He nodded to Isaac to pull away and waved goodbye. It was the last buggy to leave for the day, and he watched as it slowly ambled down the gravel lane.

This had definitely been a day to be thankful to the *gut* Lord. Each day he got to spend with those *wunderbaar* children was a day to be thankful.

When the buggy was no longer in sight, his thoughts strayed to Elizabeth. He wondered what was so important that she had taken him aside and requested a private moment. She had smiled and hadn't seemed worried or upset. Maybe it would be good news of some kind and he could add it to the things to be grateful for today. There had been enough bad news lately. Too much.

Patting his own groaning, overfed stomach, he turned and went in search of Elizabeth. A walk would do him good. And a walk with Elizabeth would ease not only his stomach, but also his heart.

Elizabeth spun around as Thomas approached her on the porch.

"I'm sorry," Thomas said. "I didn't mean to startle you. I should have stomped my feet or coughed or something."

She grinned. "Not your fault, Thomas. I'm finding myself jumping at anything and everything."

He stepped closer. "It was a *gut* day, *ja*?"

She nodded.

He stepped even closer and clasped her hand in his.

"But the day's not over." He glanced at the sun as it began its descent behind the trees, leaving long streaks of red and orange and gold in its wake. "I do believe I was asked to accompany a certain young woman on a walk. We should go now before it gets dark."

She smiled into his eyes. "Let's do it."

Hand-in-hand they stepped off the porch, strolled across the yard and moved into the nearby field. The snow crunched beneath their boots and the chill in the twilight air put a rosy glow on their cheeks.

They rehashed the afternoon's events and conversations as they walked. Elizabeth knew the Amish rarely gave compliments to anyone, but Elizabeth bragged about the two softball hits she'd seen Benjamin get. He couldn't help the wave of pride he felt for his *sohn*. And he didn't hold back complimenting her on the chocolate-and-marshmallow dessert she had surprised everyone with.

Thomas reveled in both the conversation and the walk.

It had been a very long time— -years—since he'd taken a stroll with a woman after an evening meal. Yet, here he was. Strolling. Talking. Smiling. And doing it with Elizabeth. Something he would have never believed possible.

Sometimes hurts and regrets from the past threatened to surface and spoil the moment. But he'd mentally remind himself of all the good years he had spent with Margaret. If things hadn't happened the way they did, he wouldn't have had those years—or the children, who were the fruit of that union. He had finally chosen to forgive Elizabeth. What had happened years ago had happened. He might never understand why she'd made the choices she had, but so be it. She needed his help now and that was all that mattered.

Thomas smiled. He was glad he wasn't *Gott* and wondered why anyone in their right mind would ever try to apply for the job. Controlling lives was a full-time and difficult chore.

The sun had almost set and night was not far behind.

"It is time we go back to the house." He didn't want to break the peaceful moment or bring up a sore subject, but felt he had no choice. "I don't think it wise for you to be outside once it is dark."

She agreed but her steps faltered and he sensed her hesitation.

"Elizabeth?" He stopped and faced her. "You have something you want to tell me? I find it is always best to just say what is on your mind. *Ja?*"

Elizabeth took a deep breath. Whatever it was weighed heavily on her. He wondered if he should be concerned. When she looked up at him, her eyes glistened with unshed tears.

"I'm sorry, Thomas, that I hurt you so badly." She released her hand from his. "I never meant to." She clasped her hands together tightly. "I mean I knew you'd be hurt when I left. We both would. But I had no idea how much."

* * *

Elizabeth studied Thomas to gauge the impact of her words. His posture stiffened and his body language told her he was battling to keep calm and appear unruffled. He looked like he wanted to say a thousand things but he refrained. When he did speak, he simply shrugged. "It was a very long time ago, Elizabeth. There is nothing we can do about the past."

"Ja." She reached out and gently touched his arm. "But the wounds haven't healed yet. For either one of us."

His eyes shifted and he couldn't seem to look at her. He spoke quietly and gently, but she knew raw emotion tumbled inside him. He touched her cheek and smiled into her eyes. Then he lowered his hand. "I loved you, Elizabeth. That's why it hurt so much. You left with nothing more than a scribbled note saying goodbye, no explanation or reason, and that you hoped I'd have a good life. You didn't respect me enough to tell me in person. You left a note after the fact so I couldn't try and talk you out of it. Your parents had to give it to me."

Repressed anger and hurt surfaced in his voice and it broke her heart.

"I deserved better." His eyes couldn't hide his pain.

"Ja, you did."

He didn't seem to know what to say to that. Finally he looked her straight in the eyes and asked the question that she knew had troubled him for years.

"Why, Elizabeth? What terrible thing did I do to chase you away? I thought we loved each other. Was I the only one who felt that way?"

Unable to hold back the tears anymore, she shook her head until she could clear the sob from her throat and find her voice.

"I left because I loved you, Thomas. More than you realize."

He threw a hand in the air. "That makes no sense."

"I wanted you to have a good life and I knew I couldn't give it to you. You think it is cowardice to run away. Sometimes it is courage. Sometimes you love another person so much that their happiness means more to you than your own. You're not running away, Thomas. You're crawling away because your heart is shattered into a million pieces and you can barely move. That's how much I loved you. And that is why I left." She stretched up on her toes and kissed him. The salty taste of her tears mingled on their lips.

FIFTEEN

Thomas didn't say anything. He smiled at her with all the tenderness he could muster. There were so many questions and he was grateful that she was finally ready to give him the answers he craved. But not here. Not in the dark in the middle of a field when a known predator hung in the shadows.

"We have to get you back inside. It is not safe."

She didn't protest when he clasped her hand and led her back to the house.

When they walked through the door, Mary looked up from her sewing. One glance at the expression on her face and Thomas knew she was aware of the conversation they'd been having. He'd believed for years that she'd known the real reason Elizabeth had left, but he'd never been able to get her to tell him.

"If you don't mind, Mary, Elizabeth and I are going to go into the kitchen to talk. Would you like me to bring anything out to you?"

Mary smiled. "No, Thomas. I had plenty to eat and drink today. If you don't mind, I'll sit here and finish my sewing. Elizabeth knows where everything is."

He acknowledged her statement with a nod and led Elizabeth into the kitchen.

Elizabeth put on a kettle for tea. She seemed more nervous standing in a well-lit kitchen baring her soul than she did in a twilight-dimmed field.

He hurried to reassure her. "*Denki*, Elizabeth. I am grateful you are willing to talk to me about this. I have had many questions for many years." He sat at the table and pulled her down into the chair beside him. "I still don't know why you made the choices you made—and I want to understand." He clasped her hand on the tabletop. "Tell me everything."

When she began talking it was as if a dam broke. The words tumbled out fast.

"Do you remember that I had to go into the hospital for an operation?"

"*Ja*. You had a cyst on your ovary. I visited you every day."

"Yes, you did."

"The surgery went well. I even remember the nurses had you up and walking the hospital halls the same day."

"True. What you didn't know was what the doctors found during the operation. They had to remove my right ovary because it was riddled with cysts and ineffective. But the left ovary had problems, too. I have a condition called endometriosis."

"What is that?"

"A medical condition that changed everything between us."

"I don't understand."

"Think of it as having a weed, the worst weed, growing in your fields. You can try to cut it out but you can't get it all, it keeps coming back, and it chokes your crop."

He sat quietly and listened.

She pulled her hand away and folded both hands in front of her. "Endometriosis is my weed. It is choking my insides. It is making it impossible for me to have a child." She took a deep breath. "Amish people love large families. And I knew how good a *daed* you would be. I couldn't stay here and marry you. I couldn't deprive you of a family, Thomas. So I left."

Thomas's mouth gaped open in shock. "That's why you left? Because of your health?"

Elizabeth nodded.

"But I would have married you anyway. Didn't you know that?"

She smiled at him and reached out to stroke his hand. "I knew you would because you are a *gut* man. That's why I didn't tell you. I didn't want to ruin your life."

"You should have spoken to me about this."

Thomas tried to control his anger but it was getting harder by the second. "If I had had a medical condition or maybe been injured and couldn't work the farm, would you have left me?"

"Neh," she said softly.

"Why? Because you are a better person than me?"

"Neh, Thomas. I loved you. I would have stayed by your side always."

"That's my point, Elizabeth."

She lowered her eyes and seemed unable to face him.

"You made the choice for both of us and you had no right to do that. You are not *Gott* and yet you try to control others as if you know what is best for them."

Seven years. She threw away seven years of their lives together—and for what?

He struggled with a myriad of emotions, not knowing what to say or how to act.

"I'm sorry, Thomas. I should have told you. I should have given you the choice or, at the very least, let you understand why I was leaving. I hurt you. More than I thought I would. More than I ever wanted to." Her eyes pleaded with him to try and understand. "If it is any consolation, you are not the only one who suffered. These past seven years have been difficult for me, too."

He realized she was right.

Yes, he'd been hurt. But he'd also been able to

move on. *Gott* blessed him with Margaret and then added the gift of two *kinner*.

What had Elizabeth gained?

She'd been apart from him. But she'd also been apart from her family, her friends, her community. She hadn't even been able to attend her own father's funeral and he knew that loss still cut deep.

She'd made a foolish decision but he understood now that she'd done it out of love, not malice. And she'd paid a heavy price. It wasn't his place to hold grudges against her—not anymore.

A sense of relief washed over him. He realized that this month together, keeping her safe from harm, had helped him come to grips with his pain. He'd been able to forgive her even before she'd told him the truth tonight.

He stood, came around the table and pulled her to her feet. He swept a strand of hair off her cheek. "You have nothing to be sorry for, Elizabeth. You did what you thought was right at the time. It is over. It can't be undone." He folded her in his arms. "But we can both learn from past mistakes. We must trust one another. We must be open and talk with each other. No more secrets."

Elizabeth smiled and when she did it was like a ray of sunshine peeking out from behind a dark cloud.

"*Denki*, Thomas."

"*Neh. Denki* to you. You have answered questions that bothered me for years. Now I know the truth. Now I am at peace with it."

"*Mamm* was right." She glanced over Thomas's shoulder. "Don't ever tell her I said that, though, or I'll never hear the end of it." She chuckled. "She said if I told you the entire story that we both would have something to be grateful for on this Thanksgiving Day."

He leaned forward and claimed her lips. When the kiss ended, he tilted her chin and smiled into her eyes. "*Ja*, Mary is right. I have much to be thankful for on this day. *Gott* is *gut*."

"Ahem."

Both of them jumped and pulled apart.

"Levi, I didn't see you standing there," Thomas said.

"Obviously not." The man grinned from ear to ear. "I have *kumm* to do my watch shift. You can leave now." His grin widened. "If you want to, that is."

Elizabeth giggled like a schoolgirl and the sound of it warmed his heart. "Levi is right, Thomas. The *kinner* will be waiting for you. I am in good hands."

Thomas shot a look between them. "Fine." He stepped close to Levi and lowered his voice as he passed. "Don't take your eyes off of her."

Levi, one of the younger single men in their community, grinned again. "Don't worry, Thomas. I will care for her as if she was my own."

Thomas raised an eyebrow. "Don't get any crazy ideas in your head. Just keep a careful watch."

Both Levi and Elizabeth laughed.

"Go home, Thomas." Elizabeth stepped forward and gave him a peck on the cheek. "I will see you tomorrow."

Grumbling under his breath, Thomas planted his hat on top of his head, grabbed his coat and headed for the door.

Elizabeth sat on the bed combing out her hair when she heard a knock on her bedroom door.

"Come in." She smiled as her mother entered the room. She'd wondered how long it would take her to come and pepper her with a dozen questions. She was surprised the dear woman had waited this long.

"I brought you an extra quilt." She laid it at the foot of the bed. "It might get very cold this evening. Thomas said he thinks we will soon have more snow."

Elizabeth grinned. She knew what her *mamm* wanted and it had nothing to do with keeping her warm. She couldn't resist stringing her along just a little longer.

"*Denki.* I will be warm as toast."

Her mother stood in the middle of the room looking awkward but not making any effort to leave.

"Would you like me to help you comb your

hair?" her mother asked. "I used to do the back for you when you were a teenager. Remember? We had some of the best conversations during those special mother-daughter times."

Elizabeth couldn't hold back any longer and laughed out loud. "No, *Mamm*, I don't need help with my hair." She patted a place on the bed beside her. "But you're welcome to *kumm* and sit beside me. It is a *gut* night for a mother-daughter talk."

Her mother didn't need a second invitation. She plopped on the bed, folded her hands on her lap and got straight to the point.

"You told Thomas."

"Ja."

"I thought so. And how did he take it? What did he say?" Her mother looked intently at her, clearly anxious to hear every detail.

Elizabeth laughed again. "Weren't you standing in the hallway straining your ears to hear every word?"

Her mother's cheeks colored.

She had been standing in the hall!

Elizabeth hugged her mother and laughed with abandon. "I was only kidding but you really did creep into the hallway and try to listen, didn't you?"

Her mother pulled out of her arms and tried not to appear as flustered as she really was.

"I'm sorry. I couldn't just sit there with my sewing and pretend I didn't know what was going on." She looked chagrined. "But if it's any consolation, I couldn't hear a single word. And then Levi came in and caught me snooping and I had to rush back to my chair before he made an issue of it."

Elizabeth's grin was so wide her face hurt.

"What do you want me to say, *Mamm*? That you were right? That I should have told Thomas the entire truth in the beginning? That nothing good comes from secrets?"

Elizabeth threw her hands up in the air. "Well, you were right, *Mamm*." She hugged her mother again. When she released her, she smiled into her eyes. "*Denki, Mamm*. You gave me good advice."

Her mother smiled back. "How did Thomas react? Was he upset? Angry?"

"Maybe a little…at first." She pleated her hair into a braid that hung down her back. "I'd hurt him. Deeply."

Her mother nodded.

"But eventually he understood my choice even if he didn't agree with it." Elizabeth smiled. "He forgave me." She looked at her mother and said, "And then he kissed me."

Mary's mouth dropped open. Then she grinned and clapped her hands. "See? I was right. I told you Thomas is a *gut* man. I knew he would forgive you."

Elizabeth leaned to the side and purposely bumped her mother. "And Levi caught us."

Her mother laughed and the two of them giggled like schoolgirls. It brought back memories—good memories—and Elizabeth wished she had never left home. This was where she belonged, with her *mamm*, with the new friends she was making in the community and with Thomas. Suddenly the whole world seemed filled with opportunities and she couldn't remember ever being happier.

"Well, I am glad, child, that you did the right thing. Now it is no longer a secret. Wounds can heal. And who knows what *Gott* has in store for the two of you."

"Whoa, *Mamm*. Don't get ahead of yourself. Just because Thomas and I had this conversation and he said he forgave me, doesn't mean that we will be anything more than good friends."

Elizabeth crossed to the window and reached up to pull the curtain closed.

"Good friends who kiss each other," her mother teased.

Elizabeth chuckled. "*Ja*, I must admit the kissing part was fun. I wouldn't mind trying that again."

Elizabeth tugged again on the curtain but it stuck and wouldn't slide across the wooden rod. "What's with this curtain?" She looked up, couldn't see anything in the way and tugged it again.

"We need a new rod. There's a little spur on

the top and if you don't pull it just the right way, the material gets stuck." Her mother came toward her. "Here, let me show you."

Mary stepped in front of Elizabeth and reached up to twist the material.

At that exact moment the window exploded and shards of glass flew everywhere. Both Mary and Elizabeth cried out and fell to the floor.

Elizabeth covered her face with her hands to protect against the flying glass. And she could feel little slivers bite into her hands, her neck and the little unexposed skin of her face.

Disoriented and confused, she sat up. She instinctively brushed the splintered glass off her face, shoulders and chest, while her mind tried to process what had happened. She was shaking broken glass out of her hair when she looked over at her mother.

Mary lay in a crumpled heap on the floor.

For a moment, Elizabeth thought she had curled into that position to shield herself from the flying glass.

"Mamm?"

When she didn't answer or move, Elizabeth quickly crawled across the few feet to her mother's side. Gingerly, she placed her hand on her back. "Are you *allrecht*? Did any of the glass cut you?"

She heard the thundering sound of someone racing up the stairs.

"Mamm?"

Gently, Elizabeth eased her mother over onto her back.

Her hands flew to her face and she screamed at the same moment the bedroom door burst open and Levi rushed into the room.

"What happened? What's going on?" Levi hurried to their side.

Her mother's blood smeared Elizabeth's face and covered her hands. "It's *Mamm*. I think she's dead."

SIXTEEN

Thomas hurried down the hospital corridor with Rachel clutched in his arms as he dragged Benjamin as fast as his little legs would go.

He hated hospitals.

He didn't know if it was the fluorescent lighting that always seemed unnatural and too bright, or the smell of antiseptic mingling with illness, or the sound of tears and hushed voices from the rooms he passed.

He had visited several members of the community over the years within these walls. And he had sat by Margaret's bed in this place and held her hand as she died.

Neh. He definitely did not like hospitals.

As he reached the final corridor, the waiting room came into view. His eyes found Elizabeth immediately. She sat slightly apart from the others, head bowed. Not far from her was Levi, as well as Bishop Schwartz and his wife, Sarah, and Isaac and Rebecca. The bishop had called him on the cell phone he was allowed to keep for business. He told Thomas to come to the hospital immediately. When asked why, he'd said only that Mary had been hurt and he would give him the details when he arrived. Then the bishop had told him where they would be.

Apparently Thomas was the last to arrive. But no surprise there. His farm was the farthest from the hospital and none of the others had two sleepy children to wake up and get dressed. But he was here now. His heart galloped in his chest, whether from the anxiety of having to hurry or the fear of what awaited him, or both, he wasn't sure.

Rebecca spotted him immediately and came down the hall toward him, while Benjamin let go of Thomas's hand and ran to join the others in the waiting room.

When Rebecca reached his side, she lifted Rachel, who had fallen back to sleep during the buggy ride, from his arms. "Give her to me, Thomas. Isaac and I will take care of the *kinner*. You will have other things you must do."

Rebecca glanced over her shoulder and when she turned back, she lowered her voice. "Go to her, Thomas. She needs you now."

"I will. But first, how is Mary? What happened? Is she ill? Did she have a heart attack or a bad fall or what?" he asked.

"Somebody shot her."

"What?" Shock roared through his body like

a tsunami. "Who? How?" His thoughts flew in a million different directions. He felt helpless and confused—and angry to the bone. He shook his head as if that would make it all disappear.

"Where is Mary now?" he asked.

"She's in surgery. It is bad, Thomas. The doctor told us he would do his best but we should prepare ourselves for the worst."

Thomas tried to absorb the information. "I don't understand. How did this happen?"

Before she could answer Thomas peered around her and saw the sheriff standing next to Elizabeth. He was asking her questions and writing her answers in his small notepad.

His eyes shot back to Rebecca. "It's that man Dolan, isn't it? He's back. Did he shoot Mary?" He was shocked. "Why would he do that? What did Mary ever do to him? She was no threat."

"We don't know for sure it was him. There were no witnesses, but who else would do such a thing?" Rebecca glanced back at the sheriff then returned her attention to Thomas. "The sheriff believes it was Mr. Dolan. He called his people to put out an alert."

Thomas gritted his teeth. "Tell me what happened."

"Elizabeth was at her bedroom window. She tried to pull the curtain closed but it got stuck. Mary came over to help. She stepped in front of Elizabeth just as a bullet smashed through the glass."

Thomas's stomach turned over.

That bullet was meant for Elizabeth!

"Was Elizabeth hurt?"

"Some cuts on her face and hands from flying glass. A bruise from hitting her knee when she fell onto the wood floor. But nothing serious." Rebecca looked sad and concerned. "Elizabeth's wounds go much deeper than the physical ones."

Dear Lord, denki for sparing Elizabeth. Please, Lord, don't let Mary die in her place. Mary is a gut woman, still young, and one of your faithful servants. She has had much heartache in her life. Please spare her an early death.

Thomas took one long look at Elizabeth's bowed head, her slumped shoulders and her hands covering her face.

Lord, we both know if Mary dies that Elizabeth will never be able to forgive herself. Please, Lord, be merciful.

Thomas remembered not too long ago having a conversation with Elizabeth about how he was human and he had feelings. Well, he had feelings now. Deep, dark ugly ones. He hoped the sheriff found this horrible man before he did.

"Tell me about Mary. Where did he hit her? How bad were her injuries?" He took a deep breath, trying to steel himself for the answer while his mind screamed out against the scenario unfolding right in front of him.

Mary. Shot?

He couldn't wrap his head around it. He loved Mary like another mother.

Rebecca answered honestly and directly. "From what I was told, Mary stretched her arm over her head to reach the curtain. The bullet entered through her side under her arm. The doctor said it barely missed her heart. It did splinter a piece of her sternum and the fractured bone pieces caused additional damage to other tissue as well. She lost much blood before we were able to get her to the hospital."

When Thomas looked over again, he saw that the sheriff had left. He stared at the back of Elizabeth's bowed head for several long moments. She looked frail, broken, almost as if something as soft as a whisper could blow her over. His heart ached for her. But he couldn't go to her. Not yet. Not with all these dark, angry feelings roiling inside.

He glanced at his sleeping daughter, who was nestled in Rebecca's arms, and it brought a ghost of a smile to his lips. There was still good in this world.

He placed a hand on Rebecca's shoulder. "*Denki* for taking care of the *kinner* for me." He turned and started to walk away.

"Wait!" Rebecca said in a hushed voice. "Thomas, where are you going? You should be with Elizabeth. I believe your presence will be a calming influence on her."

Thomas smiled fondly at his former mother-in-law. She had never questioned his feelings for this new woman in his life or even that he had any, which was more than he could say for himself. She had never shown any signs of remorse or jealousy that Margaret might be replaced in his heart, in his *kinner*'s heart. But then, his mother-in-law seemed to know what he already knew. Margaret would always have a place in his heart and a presence in the lives of his *kinner*. Still, her kindness and empathy touched him.

"You are a kind woman, Rebecca. I appreciate all you do for me."

"We are family, Thomas. We will always be family." Her eyes glistened with unshed tears.

Thomas knew Margaret was right there with them, at this very moment. He could almost feel her presence and she was very much on both their minds.

"*Ja*, Rebecca. Always."

The moment passed and Thomas glanced at Elizabeth again. She seemed to be purposely keeping the others at bay. He knew her well enough to know what was going on in her mind and in her heart. She believed she was the reason Mary was shot and she didn't want anyone else close enough to her to be hurt.

"You're right. Even if Elizabeth doesn't think she needs me, even if she tries to push me away, I need to be with her. I can't let her go through this alone. But not yet. I have someplace else I need to be."

Without another word, he turned and moved swiftly down the hospital corridor. He knew exactly where he was going and he couldn't get there fast enough. He had passed a set of double doors on his way in and took note of the small sign posted outside.

Within minutes he had reached his destination and pushed open the chapel doors.

The wee hours of the morning became dawn and then daylight. And yet there was still no word from the doctors about her mother. Elizabeth didn't think she had a tear left in her body. Her mother couldn't die. She couldn't lose her. Not now. Not when they'd just been reunited. And not from a bullet that had been meant for her.

"Elizabeth."

The sound of Thomas's voice flowed over her nerve endings like a healing balm. She turned to face him. He offered her a paper cup of hot coffee, presumably from one of the hospital vending machines. A swift look around the room showed more and more of their community arriving as the day progressed and word traveled from farm to farm and house to house.

She accepted the coffee gratefully.

"Can I get you something to eat? The hospital cafeteria's open. Isaac and Rebecca just got back from taking the *kinner* downstairs for some breakfast. It took them a little extra time. Benjamin decided to hit every button in the elevator before Isaac could stop him so they paused on every floor."

Elizabeth smiled for the first time in the past twelve hours. That was so like Benjamin. "*Neh*, I'm not hungry."

"Elizabeth, you have to have something. The last thing anyone needs is for you to get weak or sick, too."

"*Mamm* isn't sick, Thomas. She's shot. That horrible, evil man shot her." She looked up at him and wondered if her expression mirrored the shell-shocked emptiness she felt inside.

"I can't believe *Mamm* is fighting for her life from a bullet that was meant for me," she whispered.

Thomas didn't try to dissuade her. He simply sat beside her and clasped her hand, offering empathy and understanding. She didn't know how she'd be getting through all this if she hadn't been able to lean on his rock-solid calmness.

"We should hear something soon." He squeezed her hand. "In the meantime, you need to eat."

She shook her head. "I can't. Food would only get lodged in my throat and choke me." She squeezed his hand in return. "I'm *allrecht*. Truly. I'll eat when I need to."

She leaned her head against his shoulder. She

knew she shouldn't. She knew the Amish frowned on personal contact or affection in public. And she knew she had no right to assume a more personal relationship than Thomas might be willing to offer. They'd been an item years ago. That didn't mean Thomas wanted to rekindle old flames.

Still.

She needed him. She needed his strength, his presence, his fortitude.

And, thank the good Lord, he was giving it to her.

It doesn't matter right now if he is offering me friendship or if there is a possibility for more. He's here. Thank You, Lord.

She nestled closer, inhaling the faint scent of hay on his coat, which he'd thrown over the back of his chair. She absorbed the heat of his body through his flannel shirt as he drew her closer and wrapped his arm around her back.

"Thomas?"

"Ja?"

The sound of his voice rumbled in his chest beneath her ear and she smiled.

She raised her head and looked into his face.

"Why can't they find him? They know who he is. They know where he works, where he lives. He is a public figure. Many people know him. Why hasn't anyone spotted him yet?"

"They will. He cannot hide forever."

"He should have been arrested days ago." She

looked him straight in the eye. "Do you think they are really looking for him? I know they all thought it was a big joke in the beginning. That a simple Amish woman would mistakenly identify a revered senator as the perpetrator of such heinous crimes."

She gently pushed off him and sat up. "But they can't still be thinking I'm crazy, can they? They have to be looking for him, right? Especially now. How can they think that *Mamm* being shot is a coincidence or was done by someone else?"

"Shh, calm down." He pulled her close again, and wrapped his arm around her shoulders. "Of course they believe you. I spoke to the sheriff myself. They know he did this. Everyone does and they are looking everywhere for him. They will find him…soon. How can they not? He is flesh and blood like the rest of us. Someone will see him." He reached down and clasped her hands. "Will you pray with me?"

She nodded and was taken aback a little when she saw surprise register on his face. Did he think she didn't believe in *Gott*? Or did he still believe she was trying to control the world?

She bowed her head and clasped his hands.

They prayed together for a long while, fervently, and Elizabeth couldn't deny the sense of peace that descended upon her. No matter what happened, she knew it would be *Gott*'s will and that He would be by her side helping her through the hard times every step of the way. The thought calmed her more than anything or anyone. She had come home. Not just to her Amish roots. She had repented and returned to *Gott*.

"Ms. Lapp?"

Elizabeth and Thomas turned toward the man standing in the doorway. "I'm Dr. Gardner. I wanted to let you know your mother made it through the surgery. It is still touch-and-go, though. It was a much longer and more difficult surgery than we expected. There was extensive internal damage. We had to remove her spleen and a small part of her liver due to damage from the ricocheting bone fragments. But I've been told she's a fighter. I hope they were right because that's what we need her to be right now."

"Can we see her?" Thomas stood and faced the doctor.

"Only for a few minutes. Her body needs to rest so it will be strong enough to fight to recuperate."

"We understand." Elizabeth rose. "We won't stay long but I do want her to know we're here."

The doctor nodded and they followed him down the hall.

When he pushed open the door, Elizabeth just stood in the doorway. She couldn't make her legs propel her forward. Her mother looked so small and frail lying in that hospital bed. Tubes and wires seemed to be connected to every available piece of her flesh, even tubing in her nose. Two large machines on either side of the bed whooshed and beeped as they monitored her blood pressure, heart rate and oxygen levels. She had never seen her mother so vulnerable and it tore at her heart.

Thomas thanked the doctor as he left and gently guided her into the room.

Elizabeth crossed directly to the bed. She reached down and, careful not to disturb any of the apparatus, lifted her mother's hand to her lips. When she put it back down, one of her tears fell onto her mother's skin.

"Mamm," she whispered. "Thomas and I are here. You made it through the surgery. You're going to be just fine." She reached into her pocket, withdrew a white prayer *kapp* and positioned it on her mother's head. Smiling at Thomas, she said, "This will make her feel better when she wakes up. She would feel naked without her prayer *kapp*."

They stood by the bedside for a few moments longer, staring down at her pale, still form. Thomas leaned forward and planted a kiss on the woman's forehead.

Thomas's devotion, his tenderness toward her mother, touched Elizabeth's heart and she knew her eyes glistened with unshed tears at the sight.

"She loves you, you know," she told Thomas. "For an Amish woman who is not known for giving compliments, she sings your praises night and day."

Thomas chuckled. "I think she's pretty special, too."

He came around and clasped Elizabeth's elbow. "*Kumm*. We told the doctor we would not stay long." He gently steered her toward the door. They were just about to leave the room when they heard a very faint voice call out.

Elizabeth rushed back to her mother's side and grinned when she saw the woman open her eyes.

"Hi, *Mamm*." She clasped her mother's hand and, careful not to disturb the IV tubing, squeezed gently. "You gave us a pretty good scare." She leaned forward and pressed her lips against her mother's brow and then straightened. "The doctor said the surgery went well but you're not out of the woods yet. He said you have to fight to get better, *Mamm*. I know you can do it. You're one of the strongest women I know."

Mary slowly looked from Elizabeth to Thomas, blinking frequently as if trying to orient herself to her situation and surroundings, and then her gaze settled back on Elizabeth.

"What do doctors know?" she asked in a hoarse whisper. "They are not *Gott*. I have already spoken to *Gott*. I don't believe He wants me to come home yet."

Thomas and Elizabeth shot glances at each other and chuckled.

"Good to hear," Thomas said, "because I'm not ready to say goodbye."

Mary had a spasm of coughing, enough to make the monitors signal the nurse, who ushered them away from the bed and told them they had to leave and let her have her rest.

They were at the door to go when Mary spoke again.

"Thomas." He turned and looked her way. "Everyone must band together and find where this man is hiding. He must not be allowed to hurt anyone else."

Thomas nodded. "Don't worry, Mary. We are all working together—our community, the local police, the Philadelphia police. There is no place left for the man to hide."

"Promise me?"

Thomas raised an eyebrow.

Elizabeth knew her mother had surprised him as well as herself. The Amish didn't make promises. They simply said they would do something or they would not. They didn't ever want to promise something they might not be able to deliver. That would be the same as lying.

Elizabeth watched as Thomas straightened to his full height, his broad shoulders filling most of the open doorway. His eyes glittered with a fierce determination and his mouth looked carved in granite. He looked her mother straight in the eye when he spoke.

"I promise, Mary."

SEVENTEEN

"I have to go now, Thomas."

Thomas stood up from the sofa, where he'd been watching the *kinner* play with their toys on the hardwood floor.

"I still don't understand why you refuse to stay with us. Haven't you ever heard the phrase *there is safety in numbers*? You will not be safe all alone at your place."

His arm swept the room. "We have plenty of room. You can have your old room back. Stay, Elizabeth. At least until Mary is released from the hospital."

Rebecca looked up from her sewing and uncharacteristically inserted herself into the conversation.

"You might even decide to stay a little longer than planned. Once Mary is well enough to come home, she is still going to be weak and need extra care for quite a while. If you stay here, you won't have to do it all alone."

Elizabeth smiled at her. Both of the women knew it wouldn't matter where Mary stayed when she got out of the hospital. The women in the community would band together and help with her care, with housekeeping and cooking whether she was in her own home or in someone else's. That's what their Amish family did for each other.

No. Rebecca was matchmaking.

Elizabeth could see the hint of a smile on the woman's lips and took note how she was careful not to make eye contact with either one of them so as not to tip her hand.

Elizabeth's smile widened.

Considering that Rebecca was Margaret's mother, Elizabeth felt humbled and happy that the woman not only approved of her possible place in their lives, but also seemed to be inviting it, hoping Thomas would take the bait with proximity.

All the more reason for her to go.

"*Neh*, Thomas. I appreciate the offer but I want to go home."

Thomas nailed her feet to the floor with his intense gaze. "Running away again, Elizabeth?"

She bristled beneath his words and felt defensive and on guard. "That was uncalled for."

"Well? What do you call it?" Thomas asked. "You have been doing your best for days now to stay as far away from all of us as possible. You are skittish and nervous all the time. You constantly look over your shoulder and jump at the slightest sound. And yet you refuse to let any of us help you. I'm surprised you accepted the buggy ride here and actually came inside for a hot meal."

"I had no choice. I had no other transportation and I am sure you were the one responsible for everyone else being suddenly busy."

Elizabeth smiled at Rebecca. "*Denki*, for the meal, Rebecca. I hadn't eaten anything of substance for two days. I needed a home-cooked meal." Elizabeth moved toward the door. "But I really need to be getting home."

Thomas's eyes glittered like an iceberg in the middle of the ocean. His voice deepened and a tone of censure coated his words.

"You said you would never run away again." He pierced her with his gaze. "Why do I feel like you're running, Elizabeth?"

As they stared long and hard at each other, Rebecca lowered her eyes and pretended to concentrate on her sewing.

"My *mamm* is still in the intensive care unit. Do you really think I would abandon her when she needs me?"

Now, there was silence.

Elizabeth knew this had nothing to do with her mother, and only a little to do with her going back to her own house. Once Mary had opened her eyes, spoken, and seemed to be on the mend, Elizabeth had started subtly pushing away Thomas. Not because she didn't care. But because she did.

She was poison right now to anyone in her community and she had to protect them even if they wouldn't protect themselves.

But it wasn't until this moment, when she heard the anger in his tone and saw the fear in his eyes, that she realized Thomas had taken it the wrong way and believed she was pushing *him* away because she didn't care rather than because she wanted him safe. He was afraid to open up to her. Afraid she would break his trust and abandon him again without a word.

She had no one to blame but herself for that misconception.

When was she going to learn how to talk to him, really communicate, so he would know that she never, ever would hurt him like that again?

Immediately she crossed to his side, placed a comforting hand on his arm and smiled up at him. "Thomas, I am not running away. I will never run away again. I promise."

His eyes widened.

She knew those final two words held incredible weight with him. The same weight he'd given them when he'd promised Mary that Dolan would be found.

He reached out and clasped her arms in turn. "You are safer here. You are safer with me."

She cupped his face. "*Ja*, Thomas. I know I am safe with you. You would protect me with your life. I know that. I trust that."

She gave him her sweetest, most tender smile. "But I don't want that."

Elizabeth looked over at the children playing on the floor. Benjamin had built a corral out of twigs for his carved horse and cow and was playing with them. Rachel held her little plastic dog. She'd tied a piece of yellow ribbon around its neck and was playing at taking it for a walk across the hardwood floor. Elizabeth had to chuckle because it certainly looked more like dragging and banging than walking.

"Look at those precious, beautiful *kinner*, Thomas. They are your priority. They are the ones you must protect at all costs. And keeping me here, in their presence, is dangerous." She forced him to make eye contact with her. "I cannot allow what happened to my *mamm* to happen to these *kinner*, or you, or Rebecca or Isaac." She kissed his cheek. "And neither can you."

She stepped back and his tormented expression wrenched her heart. She knew he recognized the truth of her words but she knew him well enough to know he also wanted to be there for her and he was finding it difficult to do both safely for everyone.

"I'll be *allrecht*, Thomas. I can take care of myself."

"All alone?"

"I won't be alone."

He raised a brow.

"I am in *Gott*'s hands. *Ja?*" She smiled softly. "And I've given *Gott* a little bit of help. I've agreed to allow the sheriff to put me in protective custody until Dolan is captured."

He looked shocked, but as he stood mulling over her words, she saw he understood the logic of the decision.

"When did you make this arrangement? You've been with me and I haven't seen you speak with the sheriff."

"I wasn't sure how you would react so I discussed my plans with the bishop. He thought it was the safest thing to do and agreed to go and speak to the sheriff for me." Her smile widened. "Matter of fact, I expect either the deputy or the sheriff is waiting for me at my house right now. I told them I would return there to gather some of my things as soon as I had dinner here. That would give them time to prepare and..." She paused long enough to clamp control over her emotions. "It would give me time to say a proper goodbye."

Rebecca's head jerked up. She looked concerned but she didn't interrupt them.

Thomas pondered the information a little longer.

"How long do you think you will be gone?"

"Not long. As you, yourself, said Thomas, this man cannot hide much longer."

Although a frown pulled at the corners of his mouth, Thomas nodded his head.

"*Denki*, Thomas, for understanding. Please believe me, this is difficult for me, too. But I must protect the people I love. You understand that, *ja*?"

Tears surprisingly glistened in his eyes. He gave her a bittersweet smile.

"I need you to do one other thing for me," she said.

"Anything."

"I need you to check in on *Mamm* every day. Make her understand why I am not there and assure her that I am safe."

"There is no need to ask for something I will do anyway."

"And there's one other thing." She grinned. "Lend me a horse so I can get home. I will tend to him and leave him in the barn for you to pick up later."

"I can…"

"You can stay here with your family, Thomas, where you belong."

He stared at her for a long, hard minute and then he nodded. "I will get the horse ready."

He had just started to move toward the door when Rachel broke out in heart-wrenchingly loud wailing. All eyes turned toward the child.

Thomas was at her side and squatting beside her in a heartbeat. "What, darling? What's wrong?" His hands smoothed her hair while his eyes searched her for injury.

"Doggy's broken," she cried.

She held her pudgy little hands high. One part of the dog hung suspended from the ribbon she'd used as a leash and the other part of the dog was fisted in her other hand.

"That's okay," Thomas assured her. "Let *Daed* see. Maybe I can fix the doggy for you."

He took both pieces from her and looked at them strangely. "What...?"

Elizabeth moved in for a closer look.

"Thomas," she exclaimed. "That's not one of Hannah's toy knickknacks. I didn't look at it closely before. It's a flash drive."

"A flash what?"

"A flash drive! A flash drive! It's a portable computer file. You wouldn't believe the things you can store on one of these." She yanked the piece with the silver protrusion from his hand and held it up in front of her face for a closer look. She could barely contain her excitement as she bounced and spun around. "I can't believe I didn't look at this closer. I thought it was a knick-knack. Hannah had dozens of little toys she kept around. Most flash drives are flat and rectangular. I never suspected one could be inside something that looked like a toy. Unbelievable! *Denki, Gott!*"

"I don't understand. Why are you so excited over this—this flash drive thing?"

"Don't you see? This is it!" she said, tossing glances at both Thomas and Rebecca. "This is what Dolan has been looking for. Hannah must have put something incriminating on this drive. Something he knows law enforcement can use to put him behind bars for life." She whooped and hollered and both children, not sure why they were doing it, whooped and cheered with her.

She stopped her spinning and held the flash drive in front of Thomas's face. "This is our freedom, Thomas. Hannah gave us the gift of freedom." She threw her arms around Thomas and then kissed him soundly.

"Elizabeth..."

She grabbed his hand and started to pull him toward the door. "*Kumm*, Thomas. We have to get it to the sheriff right away."

"Whoa! Slow down." Thomas clasped her arm and made her sit down on the sofa. Elizabeth's excitement was contagious but he'd learned through life's experience to err on the side of caution. Until he understood what was happening, he wasn't going anywhere. "I know you're excited but I have questions."

"So do I," said Rebecca.

Rebecca came over and sat on one side of Elizabeth while Thomas sat on the other. The children, having fun with their whooping and hollering, continued to spin themselves until they got dizzy and collapsed on the floor laughing.

"May I?" Rebecca asked as she took the flash drive out of Elizabeth's hands and stared at it quizzically. "You said there are files stored on this toy?" She turned it one way, then another. "I don't understand how this can hold anything? Where would it be? How could it be of any help?"

Elizabeth reclaimed the drive and held it protectively in her fisted hand. "It's a piece of technology they use every day in the *Englisch* world. I know you don't understand, but trust me. I honestly believe this is the missing piece. This is what Hannah told Dolan I had in my possession. It has to be! There was nothing else of value in that box."

She started to spring to her feet. "I've got to get this to the sheriff."

Thomas stopped her from rising. "Wait!" When he had her attention, he said, "I agree. We should get this to the sheriff. But not before we know what, if anything, is on it."

"What?" Elizabeth shot him a puzzled look. "Why? How can we find out what's on the file without giving it to the sheriff first?"

"I have Mennonite friends that run the hardware store in town. They use a computer in their business. I will take it to my friend. John will put it in his computer for me and tell me what is on it." Thomas slid the drive out of her hand and placed it in his shirt pocket. "If you are right, Elizabeth, and this holds information about Dolan, I will make sure the sheriff gets it right away." He looked at her and his heart was heavy. She was so excited. So sure this would be the answer. How could he face her disappointment if she was wrong? He had to slow her down and buy both of them some time to think things through.

"Elizabeth, don't you think we should know what is on this thing before we hand it over sight unseen to the sheriff? It is possibly the only evidence against this man. We owe it to Hannah to be smart, be logical and do the right thing."

"Are you certain your friend can help us?"

"*Ja*, I am sure. He will be happy to do it. But that is not what concerns me." He stared into her eyes. "I'm sorry. I know you are excited and you don't want to delay, but Dolan is a prominent man in the *Englisch* world. I don't trust that it is a safe or wise thing to hand over the only proof of wrongdoing we have without knowing what that proof might be. Do you?"

Thomas could see her take a deep breath and slowly she calmed down.

"You're right, Thomas. We need to know what is on that drive. When you take it to your friend, ask him to make a copy for us. He can save it on his computer and put it on another flash drive for us. If your Mennonite friend owns a computer, he will know how to do that easily."

Thomas nodded. "*Allrecht,* I will drop you at your house and then I will drive the buggy into town to see my friend."

"*Denki.*"

"Will you care for the *kinner,* Rebecca?" Thomas asked.

"Certainly. I am as anxious as both of you to help catch this man before he can hurt anyone else."

Elizabeth grinned and sprang to her feet.

Thomas rose a bit slower. He didn't feel right about leaving Elizabeth at the house. Danger clung to her heels like a person's shadow.

"Are you certain the sheriff or his deputy will be there to keep you safe while I am gone?" he asked.

"I am sure."

"Fine. Then I will get the buggy ready." He paused in the doorway. "And if the sheriff is not at your house when we arrive, I will take you into town with me. Understand? I am in no mood to deal with your stubbornness right now."

Elizabeth laughed. "No problem, Thomas. I want to know what's on that drive as much as you do. I'm only going to the house to try and draw Dolan to me and away from you."

"That is supposed to make me feel better?" His insides twisted into knots. He didn't want to leave Elizabeth's side. But he didn't want to put his family in danger, either. And he couldn't think of any other way to find out what was on this contraption in his pocket than to leave them both. He prayed to *Gott* that he wasn't making a terrible mistake.

"Don't worry, Thomas. If the sheriff isn't there, we won't have a choice. We will have to go into town together." She clasped her hands in front of her chest, "But please—" her gaze pleaded with him "—we must hurry."

Without any further discussion, he grabbed his hat from the peg by the door and hurried toward the barn.

EIGHTEEN

"See! I told you, Thomas. Everything is going to be okay."

Thomas pulled the buggy to a stop next to the police car parked in front of Elizabeth's front porch. An officer got out as they pulled up.

"Good afternoon, Ms. Lapp." He extended a hand to help her descend from the buggy. "I'm Deputy Benson."

Elizabeth had to stifle a smile. This young man didn't look old enough to be a deputy or anything else in law enforcement. He looked like a teenager playing dress up. But the gun hanging on his belt wasn't a toy so she supposed she was in good hands.

"Nice to meet you, Deputy Benson. Thank you for helping us."

He touched the brim of his hat and nodded. "The sheriff said I'm not to leave your side. He wants you to pack a couple of bags and then I'm to bring you into the station."

Thomas leaned across the passenger seat of the buggy. "Have you checked the property, Deputy Benson? Are you sure no one is here?"

"I did."

"The barn, too?"

"Sir…"

The young deputy bristled beneath Thomas's questioning. "The barn was the first place I looked. I know how to do my job."

"He didn't mean anything by it, Deputy." Elizabeth hurried to defuse the male testosterone creating tension where there shouldn't be any. "This man has been too clever for all of us. Thomas is only trying to help."

The deputy looked over at Thomas and patted his gun. "She'll be fine. No one is going to get past me."

Thomas didn't look relieved. If anything, the lines on his brow and around his mouth deepened.

"Thomas, the sooner you leave, the sooner you'll have what we need and you'll come back." She waved him away. "Hurry, okay?"

Thomas shot one more frown at the deputy before snapping the reins, then he turned the buggy around and headed back down the gravel lane.

Maybe I'm imagining things, but that buggy sure seems to be leaving a lot faster than it got here.

Elizabeth smiled to herself. It felt good to have Thomas be protective and caring. But nothing could make her more excited at the moment than the discovery of the flash drive. She didn't know what was on it, but she had no doubt it was the missing piece. Soon this would all be over and then…

Elizabeth's smile widened as she pondered the possibilities.

"Ms. Lapp."

She turned at the sound of her name.

"Let's get you inside. You'll be safer if you're not standing out in the open." The deputy glanced around. "I've checked out the area but it is still a good idea to move you inside."

The deputy stepped to the side and swept a hand toward the house. "Besides, you have to get busy and pack. It'll be dark soon and I know the sheriff wants to get you settled in for the night."

Elizabeth nodded and preceded the deputy into the house.

Now all she had to do was stall the deputy for a couple of hours to give Thomas enough time to complete his task and get back here. Somehow she thought she had the more difficult assignment.

Thomas clicked the reins urging the horse faster.

He hadn't wanted to leave Elizabeth with that deputy. The man didn't look older than some of the teenagers working the fields. And the officer patted the gun on his hip as though that should make Thomas feel more confident in his ability to protect her.

Well, it didn't.

It had the opposite effect if truth be told. He looked like a young man dressed up in costume who itched for the opportunity to pull out that gun and use it. The officer's bravado showed no respect for the power and the responsibility of the weapon he wore.

But what choice did Thomas have? Rebecca was alone at his homestead with his precious children. Elizabeth was alone with a man-child pretending to be a cop. He was alone in a buggy on a dark road heading to a friend's house to find out what was on a toy.

Meanwhile a killer lurked in the darkness, able to strike anytime, anywhere, and there was nothing Thomas could do about it.

Tears burned at the back of his eyes. Hot tears. Angry tears. Helpless tears.

How would he ever survive if something happened to his *kinner* while he was off chasing down the files on a toy?

He clenched his teeth.

Was he doing the right thing?

An image of Elizabeth popped into his mind. The hope in her eyes. The excitement in her voice. Her certainty that the toy in his pocket held their freedom.

But what if this plastic dog was nothing more

than a toy? Or didn't hold any valuable information after all?

And, worse, what if the killer took this opportunity to make his final move?

Thomas's stomach soured.

Fear crept up his spine and almost paralyzed him. He'd never felt soul-deep fear. He'd been startled a time or two. Sure. Everyone had. And he'd had a sinking fear when Mary had been shot that she might not survive her injury because of her age. But this was different.

This fear was accompanied by a sense of impending doom, a mental preview of unbearable loss, a hopelessness unlike anything he'd ever experienced before.

His chest seized with panic and his breathing came in shallow bursts.

"Help me, *Gott*."

That's all he could say. That's all he could cry out. But it was all he needed. An inner peace came over him and filled him up from his toes to the top of his head.

No matter what happened this night, Thomas had to remember that *Gott* was the one in control and as much as Thomas loved his *kinner* and loved Elizabeth, *Gott* loved all of them more. Thomas found great solace in that belief.

As his buggy moved down Main Street he could still see lights in the office window of his friend's business.

Denki, Gott, that I got here before he left for home.

He hitched his horse to the porch railing, sprang up the porch steps of his friend's business, and pushed open the door.

John, sitting behind a desk, looked up when the bell over the door tinkled.

"Thomas. *Gut* to see you. What brings you out at this time of night?"

Thomas crossed directly to the counter housing one of the computers and John got up and met him there.

"Is everything *allrecht*?"

"It will be if you can help me." Thomas withdrew the flash drive from his shirt pocket and slid it across the counter toward his friend. "I need to know what is on this toy."

John picked up the dog and studied the metal prongs of the flash drive. "I've never seen a flash drive disguised as a toy. Where did you get this?"

"Please, John, it does not matter right now. I need to know the secrets hidden inside it, and every second that passes puts my family in grave danger. Can you help me?"

John's face blanched at the mention of danger, but he didn't hesitate. He immediately turned on his computer and slid the dog into an opening on the side of the machine. He hit a button once.

Twice. Then blinked at the screen and turned the laptop to face Thomas.

"Take a look, Thomas. Is this what you're looking for?"

NINETEEN

The deputy pushed his chair back and patted his stomach. "That was delicious, Ms. Lapp, I haven't had a home-cooked meal that good in years."

"Thank you."

He started to get up.

Elizabeth put her hand on his forearm to stop him and then pulled back. "Wait, officer. Let me refill that coffee cup for you. It'll only take me a few minutes to brew a fresh pot."

"Sorry, Ms. Lapp." He glanced at his watch. "We should have been on the road two and a half hours ago."

"I have pie." She hurried over to the counter and brought back an apple pie. "Now don't tell me you can't squeeze in a few minutes for a cup of coffee and a slice of pie."

The young man stared at the golden pastry and his conflicting emotions warred across his face. "I'll tell you what. You go upstairs and pack while I go outside and take another check around the house and the barn. When I come back, if the coffee is ready, we'll have a quick cup and a slice of that delicious-looking pie and then hit the road."

Elizabeth knew she'd stalled as long as she could and he wouldn't tolerate much more. She smiled sweetly. "It's a deal."

As soon as the deputy left, she put on another pot of coffee, ran upstairs to throw a few dresses and other needed items into a bag and made it back to the kitchen in record time.

She glanced out the kitchen window into the darkness.

Where are you, Thomas? I'm running out of ideas. Please. Hurry.

The smell of freshly brewed coffee filled the room and Elizabeth hoped the young deputy would find it enticing. If he was in such a big hurry, he should have been back by now. Maybe he was still sensitive about Thomas questioning him and was doing an extra-thorough job.

Or maybe he was on his car radio trying to explain to the sheriff why they weren't in town yet.

She finished washing the last of the dishes when she heard the front door open and close.

She wiped her hands on the towel next to the dish drainer, smiled as brightly as she could and turned to face the deputy.

"Your timing is perfect. The coffee…"

The words died on her lips as she faced Richard Dolan, standing in the doorway with a gun pointed directly at her chest.

She made a dash for the back door.

He moved faster and pushed her against the counter. "Just where do you think you're going, huh?" He grabbed her arm with his left hand and twisted it behind her painfully. "I'm tired of playing games with you. We're ending this right now." He pushed the gun into her stomach. "Am I making myself clear?"

Her heart beat double time and she nodded.

He saw her glance toward the kitchen entrance. "Looking for your policeman bodyguard to come to your rescue?" He gave her a menacing sneer. "I can't believe how long it took for him to finally come outside. What were you two doing in here all that time?" The evilness of his grin sickened her.

She squirmed beneath his hands. "Get away from me. Let me go."

The gun pressed into her abdomen harder.

"Don't worry, honey. I'm not interested in anything you have to offer. One of you Amish women tempted me years ago but it's not going to happen again."

Elizabeth's heart seized as his words reminded her of the broad scope of the crimes he'd committed against good, innocent people. Her mother had been right. This had to be Hannah's father. Her stomach turned and she thought she was going to be sick. She threw another look at the door.

"Look all you want. He's not coming, lady. You've run out of time. It's just you and me now."

His fingers dug into the flesh of her arm and he practically threw her into the closest chair. He leaned close and said in a soft, menacing tone, "Let me explain how this works. I'm going to ask you for the last time to give me the evidence that Hannah passed on to you. And, if you're smart, you're going to give it to me."

"How do I know you aren't going to kill me anyway?"

"You don't." He sat down next to her and slid the muzzle of his gun under her chin. "But it's the only chance you have." She took a breath of relief when he removed the gun and sat back in his chair. "Now, where is it?"

"You killed Hannah."

He blinked. "Are you kidding me? You know I did. You were there. What game are you playing?" He pointed the gun at her chest. "Are you just plain stupid? I'm not fooling around. Give me what's mine. Now."

Elizabeth's heart ached for Hannah. The last few moments of her life she knew she was dying. And she knew it was her own father killing her. Tears rolled down Elizabeth's face.

"Will it do any good if I say it was an accident?" Dolan asked. "I didn't mean to kill her.

All I wanted was the evidence she'd collected against me. We started arguing. She started hitting me and tried to run away. I grabbed her by the throat to stop her." A flash of remorse made him look almost human for a moment. "Do you think I wanted to kill my own daughter? I was angry and I squeezed too tight. By the time I realized it, she had already stopped breathing."

"You might have still been able to save her. If you had tried to revive her...if you had called 911."

He slapped her across the face. The blow stunned her and hot pain shot through her left cheek.

"You ruined everything!" He screamed at her, spittle from his words hitting her face. "You came in the door, saw what had happened and took off. I didn't have any time to think things through. I had to react. I went after you and by the time I got back..."

"You shot my mother, too. You almost killed her."

"You and I both know that shot was meant for you." He shrugged. "She got in the way."

"And you sawed through the ladder. You could have killed Thomas."

His face contorted with rage. "What did you expect? Did you think I was going to let you and your friends destroy me and everything I spent my entire life working for?"

He pushed the muzzle of his gun beneath her chin so hard she didn't dare move or even breathe for fear he'd pull the trigger.

He glared at her with an intensity that frightened her to her soul.

Please help me, Lord.

He took several deep breaths and then stepped back. "I thought it was over." He sank into the chair opposite her. "When the police published the composite drawing I thought I was in the clear. No one would be able to identify me from that stupid drawing. Didn't look like me at all. The box you gave me didn't have anything in it but junk. So I began to think maybe you really didn't have anything and I didn't have to worry about you identifying me. You'd already tried and it was a dismal failure."

Elizabeth, afraid to anger him more, remained quiet while he ranted.

"I went through the box you dropped in the doorway of Hannah's condo and I found the journals. I was named as her mother's rapist."

He looked at her incredulously "Rapist? Is that what Hannah believed?" He flailed his arm as he spoke, the gun moving wildly with each movement. "I was a drunken twenty-two-year-old young man. Okay, I didn't stop when her mother said no. I get that. But we were kids. Kids do stupid things. It doesn't make me a rapist."

"It does if she said no."

He straightened and glared at Elizabeth.

"I tried to reason with Hannah. I tried to explain. She wouldn't have any of it. She told me that I'd ruined her mother's life and forced her to marry a man she hadn't loved. And that I ruined her life because that man never accepted her for his own."

He waved his arm again as he spoke.

"Why couldn't she leave it alone?" He stared at her. "I convinced myself that I had the evidence against me in those journals. The composite was a joke. I was free and clear, so I went home."

Again, the gun pointed her way. "But then the police said a witness was coming forward with evidence so I realized I wasn't in the clear after all." He hit her again. "You deserve everything that is going to happen to you. We both could have gone on with our lives in peace if you didn't decide to go to the police.

"When Hannah came to my office to confront me, I denied everything. We argued. I threw her out. But not before she'd grabbed my coffee cup from my desk." He inched closer. "She had a DNA test run, didn't she? That's the evidence you're planning on using against me."

He sprang up, overturning his chair with a loud bang that made Elizabeth flinch.

"I can't let you ruin me. My marriage and family. My future run for president. My entire life hangs in the hands of a stupid, Amish fool."

He outstretched his hand. "Time's up. Give it to me. Now."

"I will." She barely moved her lips, not wanting her chin to press against the barrel of the gun.

He looked surprised for a moment. Then he grinned and moved the gun away. "Good. Now you're talking intelligently." He held out his left hand, palm up. "Where is it?"

"I don't have it on me." She threw her hands up to protect her face when she saw his angry expression. "What? Do you think I'd carry something so important around in my apron pocket? I'll—I'll get it for you."

"You better." He dragged her to her feet and shook her hard, his fingers digging into her flesh. "What evidence do you have?"

"Hannah put everything on a flash drive."

"Where is it?"

"Right here." Thomas stepped into the kitchen. His heart pounded in his chest at the sight of his worst nightmare. The armed man dragged Elizabeth to her feet and Thomas could tell from the pained expression on her face that his fingers were digging into her arms.

Neither of them must have heard the buggy pulling up, or Thomas letting himself into the house. He had a moment of self-doubt. Maybe he shouldn't have made his presence known. Maybe he should have run to the barn for a pitchfork or shovel to use as a weapon. But once he saw Dolan with his hands on Elizabeth he couldn't turn away.

And where was the deputy? He'd been right. The man hadn't been sufficient protection at all.

Elizabeth's gaze locked with his and he saw a flash of hope. But just as quickly it changed to one of fear and regret. He knew she believed Dolan was going to kill them and she didn't want him here.

Dolan pulled Elizabeth in front of him as a shield and put the muzzle of the gun under her chin. "Stay back or I'll kill her."

Thomas raised both his hands. "Relax. I'm no threat. There's no need for you to hurt anyone."

"Do you have the flash drive?"

"Ja." Thomas held up the drive in his right hand.

Dolan looked at it and then got angrier. "Do you think I'm stupid? That's a kid's toy!" Without hesitation he lowered the gun and shot Elizabeth in the shoulder.

She screamed out with pain and collapsed onto the floor.

"No!" Thomas began to move toward her when Dolan lifted the muzzle of the gun and pointed it at Elizabeth.

"Stay where you are or I'll shoot her in the head and be done with it."

Thomas froze in place, slowly raising his hands again. "This is the flash drive. We thought it was a toy, too. That's why we didn't put it in the box we gave you. I let one of my *kinner* play with it but it isn't a toy. Let me prove it."

Dolan nodded his permission.

Slowly, Thomas pulled apart the toy, revealing the flash-drive mechanism.

Dolan looked surprised, then relieved. "Give it to me."

"Gladly." Thomas threw the flash drive as hard as he could, hitting Dolan in the right eye. Dolan instinctively raised his right hand to his eye and pulled the gun away from Elizabeth while Thomas rushed forward and slammed into the man. They smashed against the counter, bounced off of it and fell entwined to the floor.

Thomas fought desperately to subdue the man while still trying to pull the gun from his hand.

As they fought, Elizabeth's hands joined the mix and she, too, tried to pry the gun away.

"Hold it! Don't move!" Deputy Benson rushed forward and placed his gun against Dolan's temple. "Give me a reason to pull this trigger."

Dolan, realizing he didn't have a chance, released his hold on both Thomas and the gun.

Thomas rolled away then squatted beside Elizabeth. "He shot you. How badly are you hurt?"

Both of them looked at the large circle of blood on the left side of her dress.

"Let me see. We need to stop the bleeding."

"*Neh*, Thomas. It'll be fine. Let's get the flash drive to the sheriff."

Red and blue strobe lights shone through the kitchen window.

"That's him, now," Thomas said. "I sent my friend to get him while I hurried back here. We have to get you to a hospital."

The sheriff, followed by one of his other deputies, barged into the room and quickly assessed the situation.

"Lie still, Ms. Lapp. I'll radio for an ambulance unless you want my deputy to take you. It will be quicker than waiting for the ambulance."

Elizabeth sat up. "No. I'm all right. I don't need an ambulance."

He helped Thomas lift Elizabeth to her feet.

She looked at Thomas. "Was I right? What was on the flash drive?"

Thomas put an arm behind her back and supported her with his strength. "A DNA report, copies of her mother's journal pages, a birth certificate. Everything you need."

Elizabeth smiled at him. "*Denki*, Thomas." Her voice riddled with pain she nodded at the sheriff. "Give the sheriff the flash drive."

He did.

The sheriff looked at the plastic dog in his hand. "Who would have thought this was anything other than a toy?" He turned to his deputy. "Take Ms. Lapp to the hospital." He gestured toward the others. "But first, cuff Dolan and put him in the back of my car. I'll take him in and book him myself."

Once the deputy dragged Dolan out of the room, the sheriff patted Deputy Benson on the shoulder. "You better go with them. Looks like the back of your head is going to need a few stitches."

Elizabeth leaned heavily against Thomas's body and smiled at the young deputy and sheriff.

It was over.

Finally.

The following morning, Elizabeth sat in a wheelchair beside her mother's bed.

"Are you sure you're going to be *allrecht*?" Mary asked.

"That's what I should be asking you," Elizabeth replied.

"They are moving me out of ICU today and into a regular room. I should be able to come home in no time."

"*Ja*, I know. I'm your new roommate. I had to have surgery last night to remove the bullet from my left shoulder. The doctor wants me to stay in the hospital for a couple more days so I asked him to put me in a room with you. I begged Thomas to bring me here to see you so I could tell you myself."

"Against my better judgment," Thomas said.

"But you know how stubborn this one can be. I figured if I grabbed a wheelchair and brought her down here for a minute, I could get her to go back to her room and rest."

"*Gut*, now go. You see I am better. They will bring me to the room soon. Go back and rest because when they move me I am going to want to hear all the details about what happened."

Thomas and Elizabeth laughed.

Neither of them spoke as Thomas wheeled her back to her room. He helped her get into bed and pulled the covers up over her sling.

Elizabeth grimaced.

"You're in pain."

"Some."

"See. The doctors know what they are talking about. You should be in bed."

"I am in bed, Thomas."

"*Ja*, and you are going to stay there. I am planning a large wedding in three weeks' time. If you keep getting out of this bed, you won't heal and I will have to marry you in your wheelchair. I don't think you will be happy."

Elizabeth blinked and then blinked again.

"What did you say?"

Thomas clasped her right hand. "You heard me. I spoke to the bishop and he gave us permission. The week before Christmas will be a perfect time for a wedding. No one else has asked for those dates."

He sat on the edge of the hospital bed, still clasping her hand in his. "Rebecca and some of the other women are already making the plans."

"Aren't you forgetting something?" Elizabeth's heart pounded against her chest. She was thrilled and scared all at the same time.

"What? That I didn't properly ask you? *Neh*, I asked you seven years ago. You haven't properly answered."

"Thomas, nothing has changed. I have endometriosis. We will never be able to have children."

"We have *kinner*, Elizabeth. Two *kinner* who need a *mumm* and already love you. Do you love them?"

"You know I do."

"Besides, I spoke with the doctor about this endometriosis. Some women are still able to have *kinner*. Maybe you will be one of those women."

"And if I can't?"

"It is not up to us, Elizabeth. It is in *Gott*'s hands. I trust whatever His plan is for our lives." He kissed her hand. "I love you, Elizabeth. I am not marrying you to breed you like cattle. I am marrying you because I have never met anyone as stubborn or independent or vulnerable and loving and kind as you. I want to spend the rest of my life with *you*. What *Gott* chooses to do with our lives, I accept."

He leaned forward and kissed her, sweetly,

lovingly. "Will you be my wife?" he whispered against her lips.

"*Ja*, Thomas, but only because you asked properly." She smiled up into his eyes. "And also because I love you. I have always loved you. And I will love you for the rest of my life." Then she leaned forward and kissed him right back.

EPILOGUE

First day of summer
Eighteen months later

"*Neh*, Benjamin!" Thomas yelled, then shook his head when he realized his words were too late. He watched his son splash in a mud hole on the side of the barn. "He's going to be seven soon. When will he start being more responsible?"

Elizabeth cupped her husband's chin and turned his face toward hers. "He is a six-year-old boy right now, Thomas. This is what *kinner* do. They play. They explore. And they get dirty."

"*Ja*, but not when we are going to church service. He knows better."

"You're right." Elizabeth reached into her bag and showed him an extra pair of trousers. "But with Benjamin I am always prepared. I'll take him inside to change. And I will be sure he knows neither one of us is happy with what he has done."

Her lips twitched as she tried not to grin.

"Elizabeth." He spoke in his sternest tone, but seeing the look on Elizabeth's face he suspected Benjamin's chastising wasn't going to be too tough.

"I know, *lieb*. It's not funny. He must stay clean at least long enough for church. He can play with the other *kinner* after service and get dirty then if he wants. I will tell him."

Thomas leaned forward and kissed her lips. "Have I told you what a good *frau* and *mamm* you are?"

"*Neh*. But I try to be."

"You are."

"*Denki*, husband."

"At least I told you how much I love you."

"*Neh*, not today."

"What? Well I have to do something about that." He stepped forward and clasped her in his arms. She fit perfectly, like a missing puzzle piece. The top of his chin rested on her *kapp*. She pressed her face against his chest.

"I love you, Elizabeth King." She smiled up at him and he kissed her, deeply, lovingly. "You have my heart."

"I love you, too" she whispered.

"Yuck! Stop it! You're squeezing me." Rachel, caught between them during their embrace, pushed her way clear of Elizabeth's skirts and moved to the side. She put her hands on her little four-year-old hips and scolded her father. "You should look and make sure I'm not standing in front of *Mamm* when you kiss her, *Daed*. You squeezed me."

Both of them laughed.

Thomas dropped to one knee. "You are right, little one." He pulled her into his arms, gave her a kiss and a snuggle, then tickled her with his beard until her giggles filled the air. "Am I forgiven?"

She threw her arms around his neck and squeezed hard "Just don't do it again. Okay?"

Thomas grinned. "Okay."

"Rachel, come with me." She took the girl's hand. "We have to get Benjamin changed before the church service begins."

Before he joined the men, Thomas stood for a moment and watched his family walk into the house. He offered a silent prayer of thanks. He didn't know why *Gott* had chosen to bless him twice with two wonderful wives in his life, but he would be forever grateful.

Benjamin behaved during the two-hour service. Elizabeth must have spoken to him. When the service ended and everyone moved outside, Benjamin looked at him and said, "I am sorry, *Daed*, for getting dirty before church. I won't do it again."

Thomas crouched down to be eye level with the lad. "You are growing into a young man now, Benjamin. You are not a baby or toddler anymore. Did your *mamm* speak to you about the mud?"

"Yes, sir."

"Then you have been corrected enough. You may go now and play tag with the other boys. We will be spreading our picnic blanket under that tree." Thomas pointed to a tree slightly away from the others in the middle of the field.

"When I wave, *kumm* and eat with us."

"Yes, *Daed*." Benjamin turned and ran off with several of his friends.

Usually the families ate together after the service, but today Elizabeth had requested they have their own picnic. She'd spoken to the other women first and got their blessing.

As he started to walk toward the field where Elizabeth waited for him, he noticed the other women watching him and giggling and whispering to each other.

He politely nodded his head as he passed them. He wished Elizabeth had not made this request. He felt awkward sitting alone in the field while everyone else gathered for a feast at the house. But she'd been insistent that she wanted to have this private family picnic and there was little he would deny her.

He plopped down on the blanket beside her. She'd already set out fried chicken, mashed potatoes and gravy, corn and hot rolls. The tantalizing aromas almost made him forget his awkwardness at being apart from the others.

Almost.

"Where is Rachel?" he asked as she handed him a plate full of his favorite foods.

"Your *mamm* has her. They are sitting with Isaac and Rebecca up at the house."

"Elizabeth, tell me again why we are eating apart from the others?" He did not want to upset her but he was getting more uncomfortable by the minute. They could have a picnic another time. Right now they should be at the tables set up outside the main house with the others.

"It's the first day of summer, Thomas. It is a perfect day for a picnic."

"*Ja*, it is a perfect day." He tossed a glance around. "Well, at least we aren't the only ones going separate from the others today."

Elizabeth shot him a questioning glance.

"Look." He pointed to the silhouettes of two people talking under a tree at the other end of the field. "I believe that is Mary and Joshua."

Elizabeth strained to see past his shoulder. "So it is." She smiled. "What do you think they are talking about that is so important it needs to be done privately?"

Thomas shrugged. "You know I am not one to gossip."

"*Ja*, but?" Elizabeth's smile widened.

Thomas appeased her. "Joshua happened to mention to me that he might not be going to Sarasota this winter. That there might be a good reason for him to stay here."

Elizabeth clapped her hands. "Oh, Thomas, that would be *wunderbaar.* My mother is still in her prime. Fifties is not old these days. It has bothered me terribly that she is all alone. Especially since she said there were enough older adults in our lives once your parents returned, and insisted on staying in her own home."

"*Ja,* that's where you get your stubbornness."

Ignoring the barb, she said, "I've liked Joshua from the moment I met him last spring, when he returned with your parents. I've been praying that *Gott* would make a path for these two people to each other." She raised her hands to ward off any chastising from him about trying to control people's lives. "*Gott* willing, of course."

Thomas shook his head and wagged his finger at her. Then he glanced again toward the house and couldn't help but notice that not just the women, but many of the men also looked their way. "Elizabeth, you are right. It is a perfect day. But I am not sure this is the perfect time for a picnic." He gestured toward the house. "Our place is with the others. We can have a picnic another time."

"I spoke to the bishop and the other women. No one minds, Thomas."

"I mind. It does not feel right." He glanced again at the community, who all seemed to be watching them.

"Don't be silly, husband. You are allowed to

have a picnic with your wife, aren't you? I made your favorites."

He took a bite of the chicken. The tender meat almost melted in his mouth.

"This is very *gut*."

"Denki."

He took another bite. "Why aren't you eating?"

"I will have some soup later. My stomach is unsettled right now."

He looked at her hard, concern making his pulse quicken. "Are you ill?"

"No, *lieb*. I am not ill." Her eyes shone and she smiled.

"I don't understand."

"Yesterday was the last day of spring and already we are beginning summer. But it has been a beautiful spring this year, hasn't it? It is the beginning of new life, Thomas. You have already planted our fields and with *Gott's* favor we will have a good harvest this year. The flowers have poked their heads through ground that is no longer frozen and the buds have blossomed. Leaves are again covering the trees. *Gott* is showing the world that nothing is impossible. Even after the dead of winter there can be new life."

He resisted the urge to touch her forehead and see if she had a fever. She had not been herself for weeks but this recent behavior was upsetting. Later today he would make a point to talk with

Mary. Maybe she would be able to help him understand why Elizabeth was acting so strangely.

"Do you understand what I'm trying to tell you, Thomas?"

He stared at her blankly.

He really wasn't happy he had agreed to this picnic. But he didn't want to upset her, either. Women. Sometimes they are so difficult. Why don't they just speak frankly and clearly like men?

He placed his plate down on the blanket. He couldn't play this game with her any longer.

"No, Elizabeth. I don't understand. I don't want to hurt you or make you angry but I should not have agreed to this picnic. We do not belong here. We belong with the others. It doesn't matter that spring has just ended and summer begins. This happens every year. This year is no different."

"Ahh, Thomas, but this spring was very different. *Gott* blessed me with new life, too. I am pregnant."

It took a moment for his mind to understand what she had just told him.

"What did you just say?" Confusion, surprise and excitement all tumbled together inside him.

"I'm going to have a *boppli*."

"Are you sure? I thought the doctors said..."

"I am sure. I have seen a doctor." She clasped his hand in hers. "You were right, Thomas. *Gott* is in control. He has a plan for our lives. And He knows better than the doctors." She stroked his check. "We are having a child, Thomas. A gift from *Gott*."

His heart exploded with joy. He wrapped her in his arms and kissed her soundly.

Thomas could hear cheering and calls of congratulations drifting across the field. It seemed he was the last one to know about this secret. He turned and waved to the others before turning his attention back to Elizabeth.

The others could wait.

He was having a picnic with his wife.

* * * * *

If you enjoyed THE AMISH WITNESS,
look for these other great books
from author Diane Burke,
available now.

THE MARSHAL'S RUNAWAY WITNESS
HIDDEN IN PLAIN VIEW
SILENT WITNESS
BOUNTY HUNTER GUARDIAN
DOUBLE IDENTITY
MIDNIGHT CALLER

Find more great reads at
www.LoveInspired.com

Dear Reader,

The national political scene was the initial in-
spiration for this story. So many politicians ran
on family values and Christian beliefs but didn't
hesitate to sling mud and ridicule their opponents
only to rally around and praise the same opponents if they were elected.

Made me think a lot about secrets and lies.

This story came to life when Elizabeth and
Thomas emerged from the recesses of my mind.
Would the Amish, famous for their family values
and deep religious beliefs, keep secrets and lies?
If so, what kind of secrets and what would be the
motivation behind them?

And, as always, most of my stories deal with
questions of trust and forgiveness because I believe each one of us is faced with these issues at
some time in our lives.

I hope you enjoy the story of Elizabeth and
Thomas as they are forced to face these issues
amid a backdrop of danger and intrigue.

I love to hear from my readers and can be
reached at diane@dianeburkeauthor.com and
also can be found on Facebook and Twitter.

Blessings,
Diane Burke

Get 2 Free Books,
Plus 2 Free Gifts—
just for trying the
Reader Service!

Love Inspired®

Get 2 Free Books,
Plus 2 Free Gifts—
just for trying the Reader Service!

◆ HARLEQUIN™

HEARTWARMING™

HOMETOWN HEARTS ♥

YES! Please send me **The Hometown Hearts Collection** in Larger Print. This collection begins with 3 FREE books and 2 FREE gifts in the first shipment. Along with my 3 free books, I'll also get the next 4 books from the Hometown Hearts Collection, in LARGER PRINT, which I may either return and owe nothing, or keep for the low price of $4.99 U.S./ $5.89 CDN each plus $2.99 for shipping and handling per shipment*. If I decide to continue, about once a month for 8 months I will get 6 or 7 more books, but will only need to pay for 4. That means 2 or 3 books in every shipment will be FREE! If I decide to keep the entire collection, I'll have paid for only 32 books because 19 books are FREE! I understand that accepting the 3 free books and gifts places me under no obligation to buy anything. I can always return a shipment and cancel at any time. My free books and gifts are mine to keep no matter what I decide.

262 HCN 3432 462 HCN 3432

Name	(PLEASE PRINT)	
Address		Apt. #
City	State/Prov.	Zip/Postal Code

Signature (if under 18, a parent or guardian must sign)

Mail to the **Reader Service:**

IN U.S.A.: P.O. Box 1867, Buffalo, NY. 14240-1867
IN CANADA: P.O. Box 609, Fort Erie, Ontario L2A 5X3

Get 2 Free Books,
Plus 2 Free Gifts —
just for trying the Reader Service!

MYSTERY **W(O)RLDWIDE LIBRARY**®